Parents!

Your child's love of reading starts here, with HarperAlley's **I Can Read** *Comics*!

I Can Read *Comics* introduces children to the world of graphic novel storytelling and encourages visual literacy in emerging readers. Comics inspire reader engagement unlike any other format. They ask readers to infer and answer questions, like:

1. What do I read first? Image or text?
2. Why is this word balloon shaped this way, and that word balloon shaped that way?
3. Why is a character making that facial expression? Are they happy, angry, excited, sad?

From the comics your child reads with you to the first comic they read on their own, there are **I Can Read** *Comics* for every stage of reading:

LEVEL **1**

Simple stories for shared reading.

LEVEL **2**

Engaging stories for children reading on their own.

LEVEL **3**

Complex stories for independent readers.

The magic of graphic novel storytelling lies between the gutters. Unlock the magic with…

I Can Read *Comics*!

Visit **ICanRead.com** for information on enriching your child's reading experience.

I Can Read *Comics* Cartooning Basics

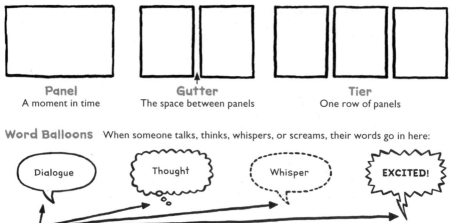

Panel	Gutter	Tier
A moment in time	The space between panels	One row of panels

Word Balloons When someone talks, thinks, whispers, or screams, their words go in here:

Dialogue   Thought   Whisper   EXCITED!

Tails
Point to whoever is talking / thinking / whispering / screaming / etc.

A quick how-to-read comics guide:

In a **panel**, read the text on the **left** first.

Then, read the text on the **right**.

Remember to...
Read the text along with the image, paying close attention to the character's acting, the action, and/or the scene. Every little detail matters!

No dialogue? No problem!
If there is no dialogue within a panel, take the time to read the image. Visual cues are just as important as text, so don't forget about them!

On a page, **start here**, in the **top left** corner!

After that, read the panel immediately to the **right**.

When you're done up there, come down here and read **this** panel next!

ME NEXT! ME NEXT!

You're almost there...

YOU MADE IT! You just read a comic page!

YAY!

HarperAlley is an imprint of HarperCollins Publishers.
I Can Read® and I Can Read Book® are trademarks of HarperCollins Publishers.

Baby Shark: Luck of the Claw
© The Pinkfong Company, Inc. All Rights Reserved. Pinkfong™ Baby Shark™ and Baby Shark's Big Show!™
are trademarks of The Pinkfong Company, Inc., registered or pending rights worldwide.
© 2023 Viacom International Inc. All Rights Reserved. Nickelodeon is a trademark of Viacom International Inc.
Printed in the United States of America. No part of this book may be used or reproduced in
any manner whatsoever without written permission except in the case of brief quotations
embodied in critical articles and reviews. For information address HarperCollins Children's
Books, a division of HarperCollins Publishers, 195 Broadway, New York, NY 10007.
www.icanread.com

Library of Congress Control Number: 2022944211
ISBN 978-0-06-315896-2

Book design by Elaine Lopez-Levine
23 24 25 26 27 LB 10 9 8 7 6 5 4 3 2 1   First Edition

I Can Read! Comics
LEVEL 1

pinkfong
BABY SHARK™

Luck of the Claw

STEVE FOXE   JASON FRUCHTER

HARPER
alley

An Imprint of HarperCollinsPublishers

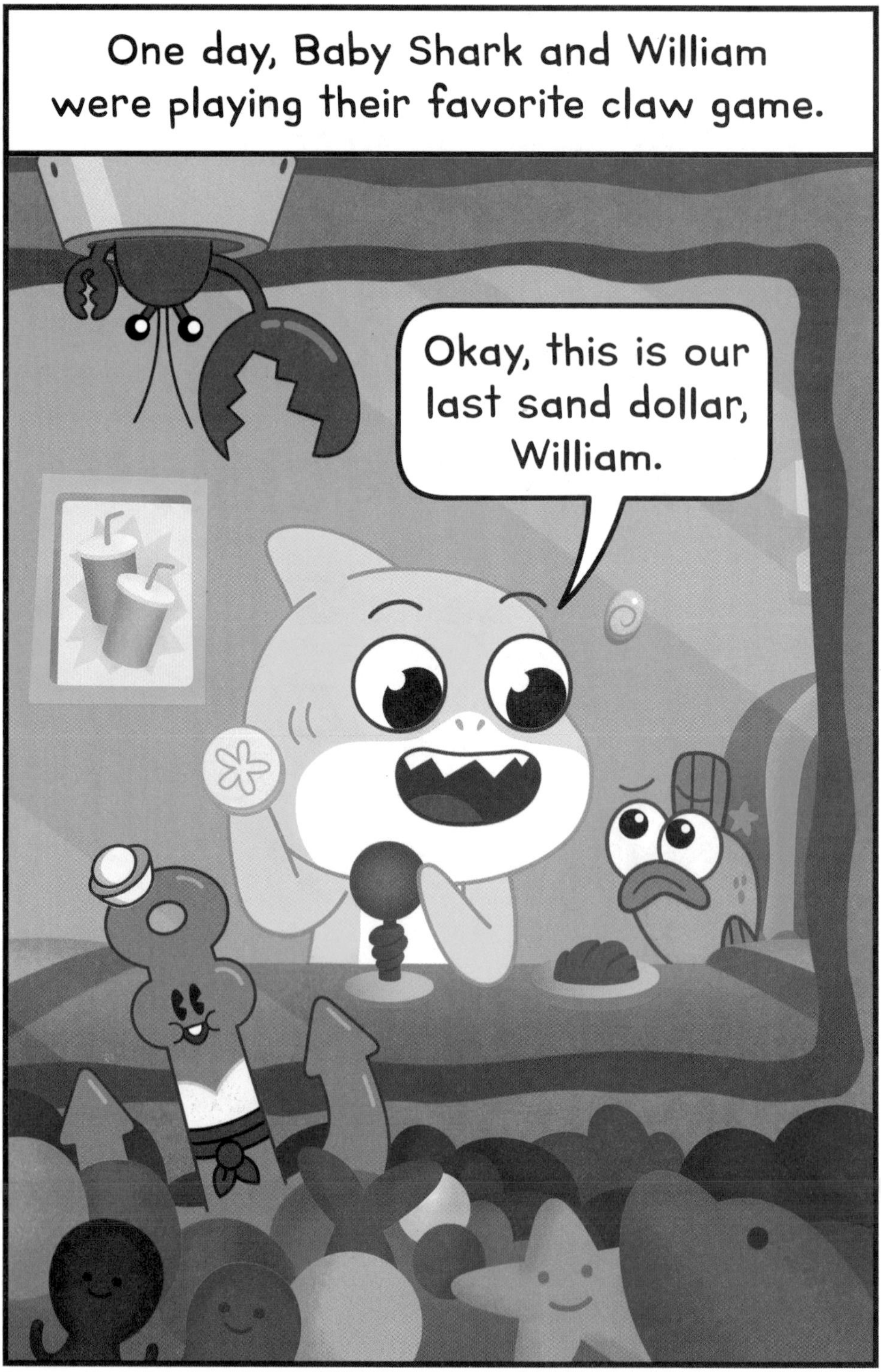
One day, Baby Shark and William were playing their favorite claw game.
Okay, this is our last sand dollar, William.

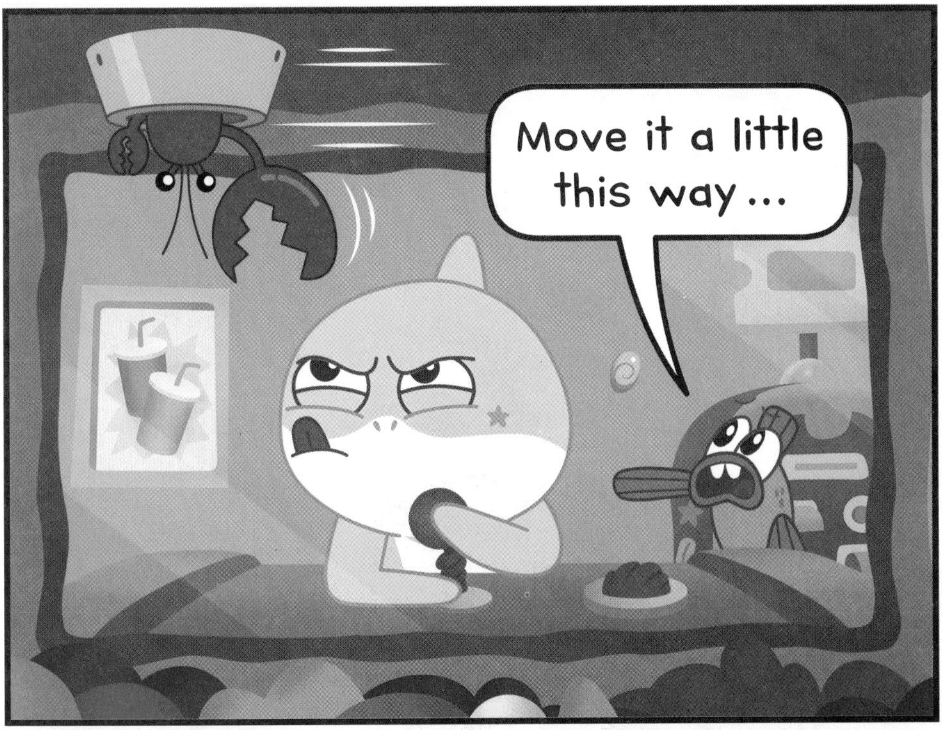
Move it a little this way ...

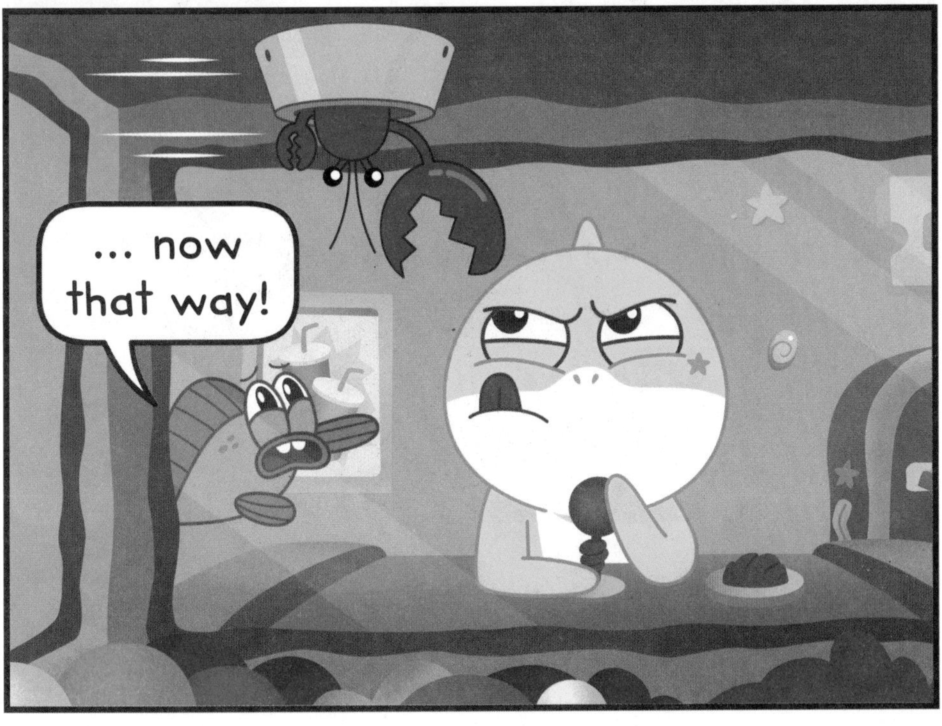
... now that way!

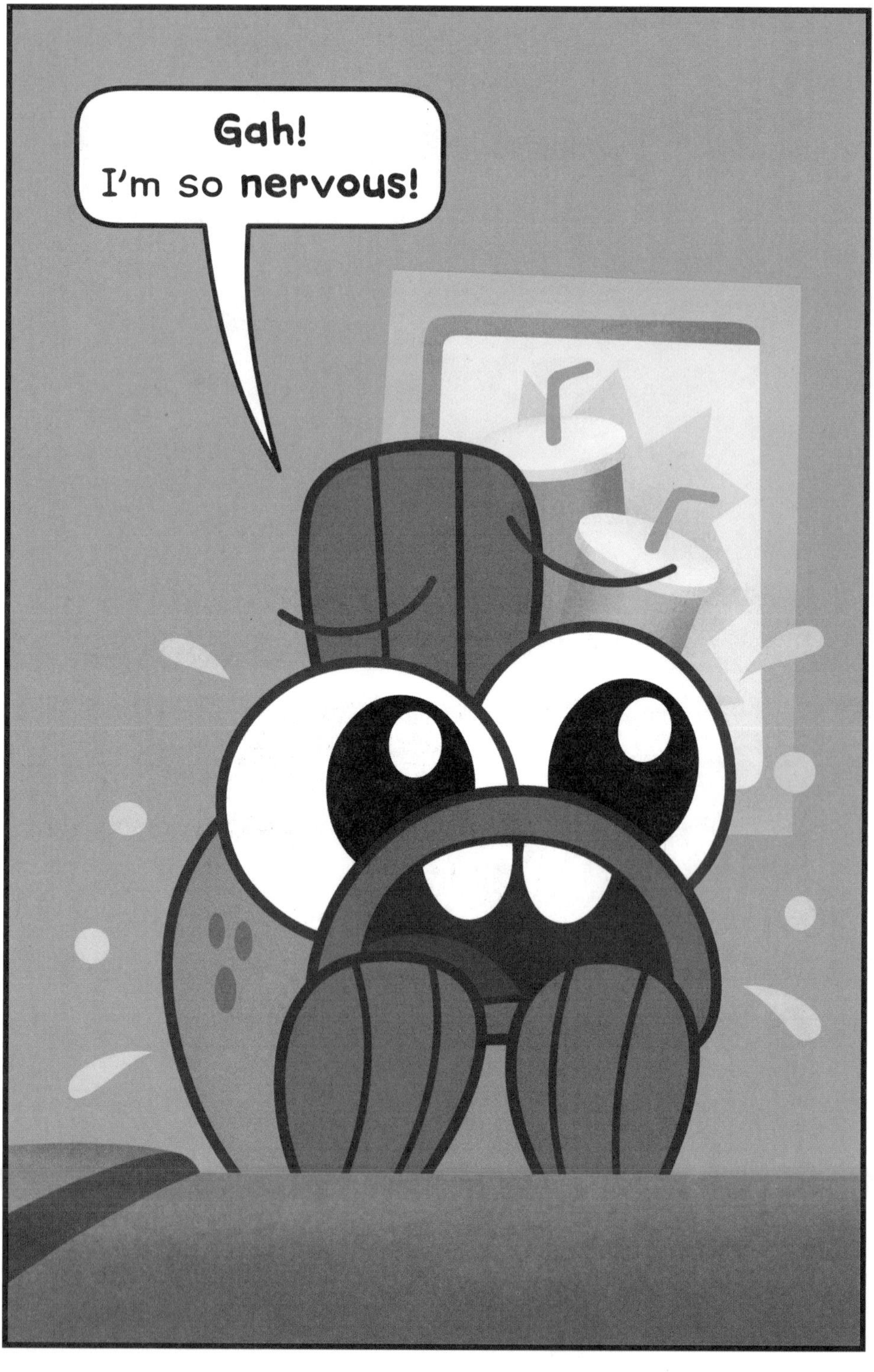
Gah!
I'm so **nervous!**

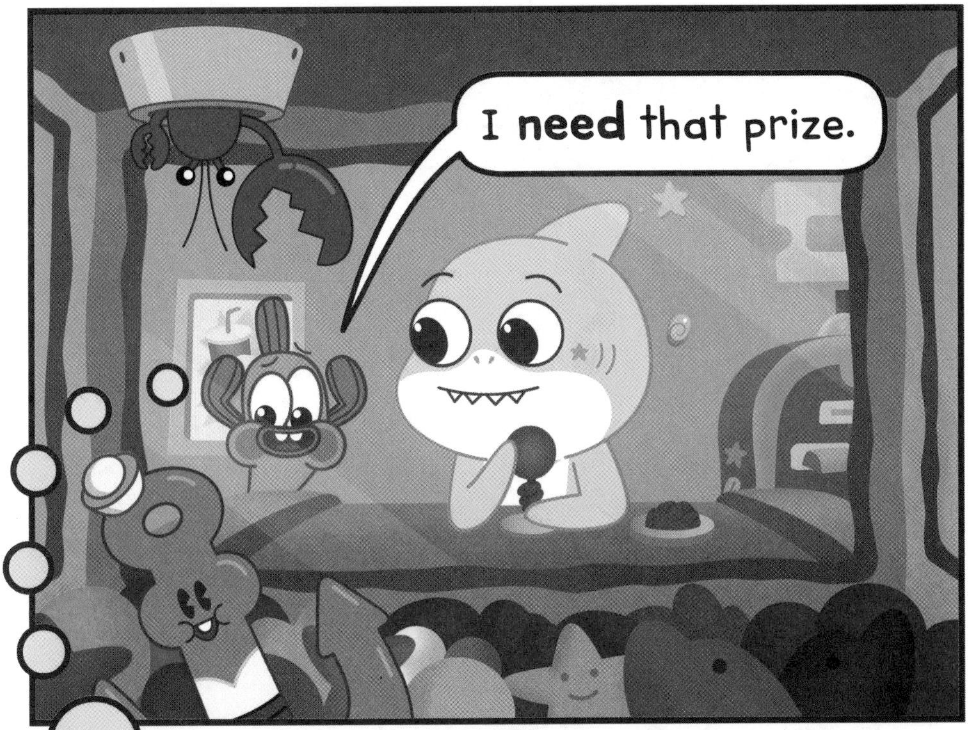
I **need** that prize.

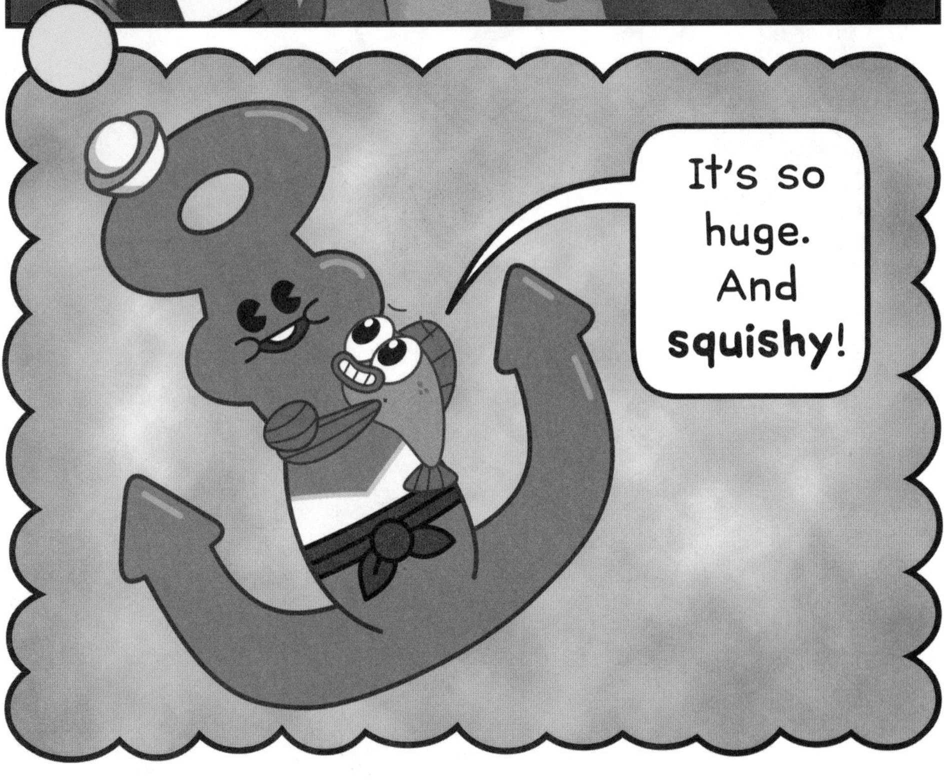
It's so huge. And **squishy**!

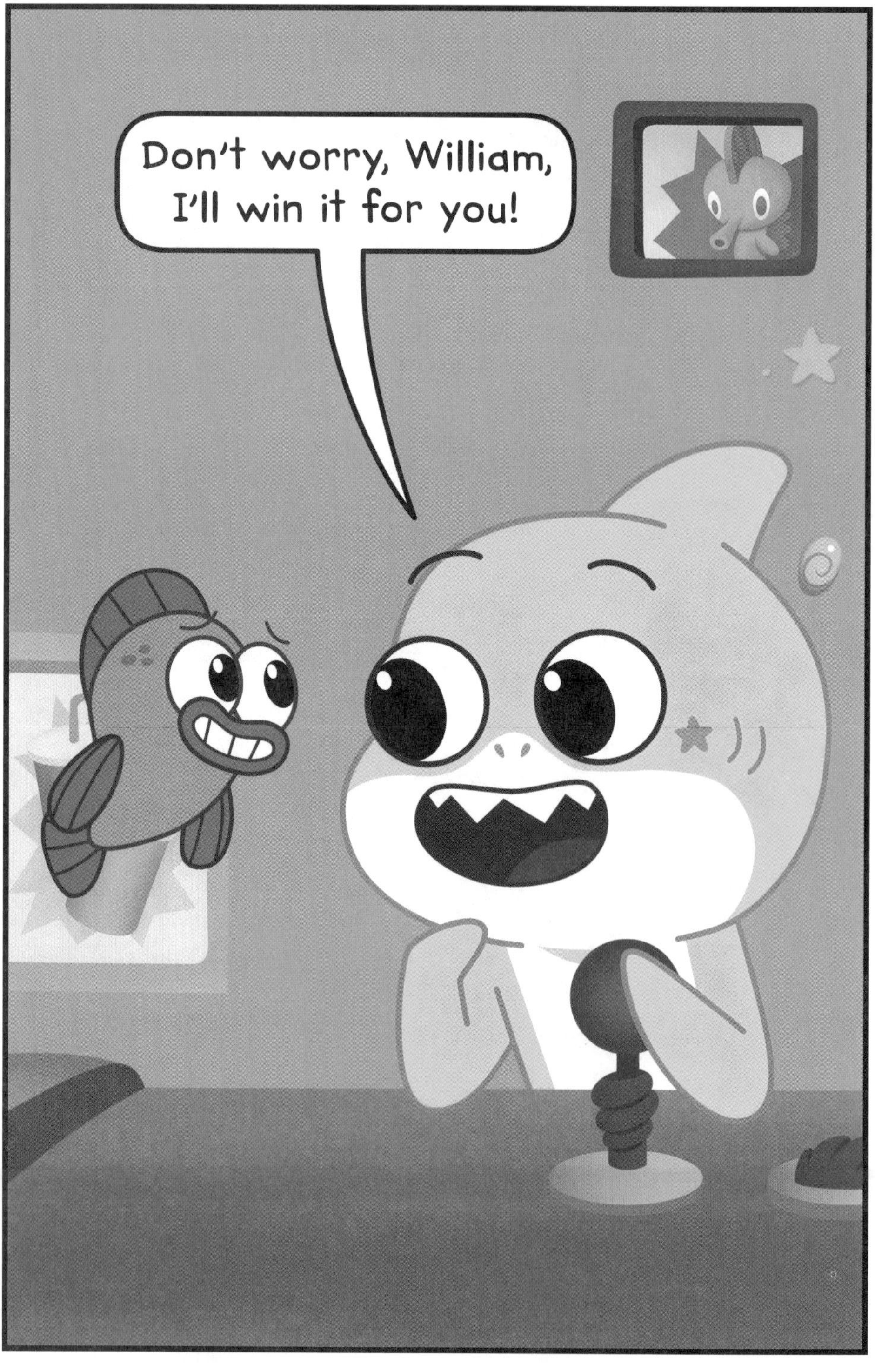
Don't worry, William,
I'll win it for you!

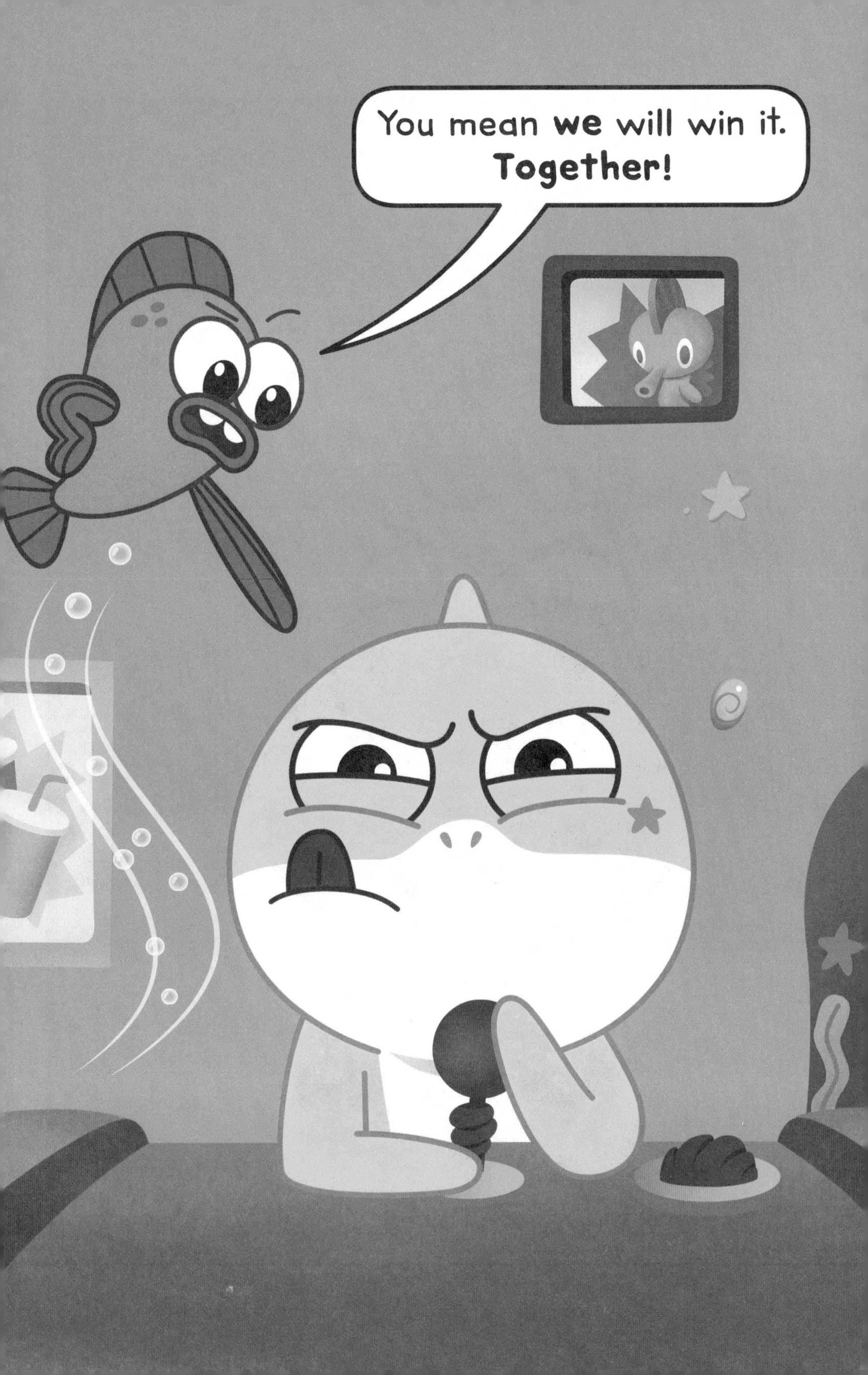
You mean **we** will win it. **Together!**

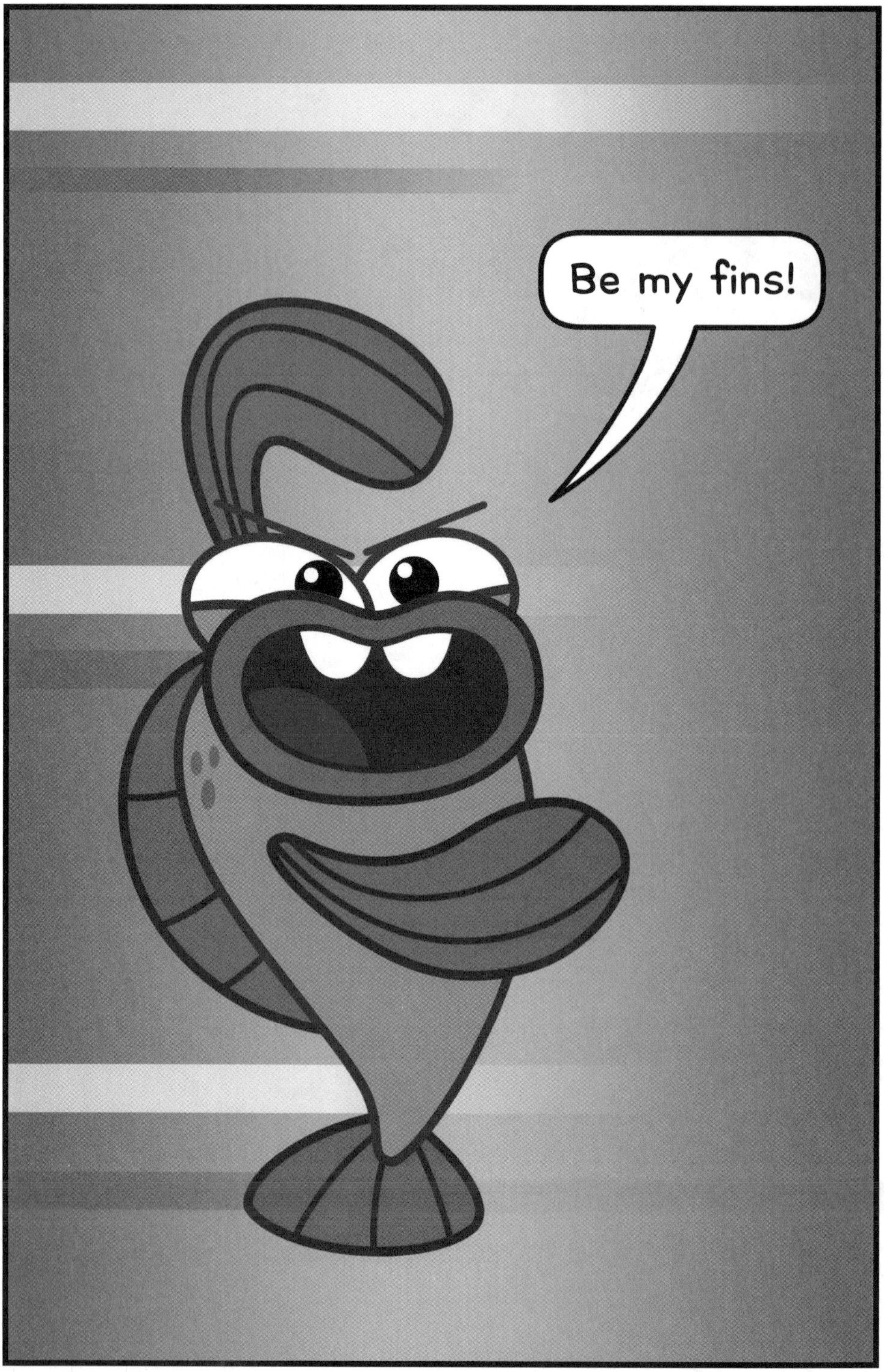
Be my fins!

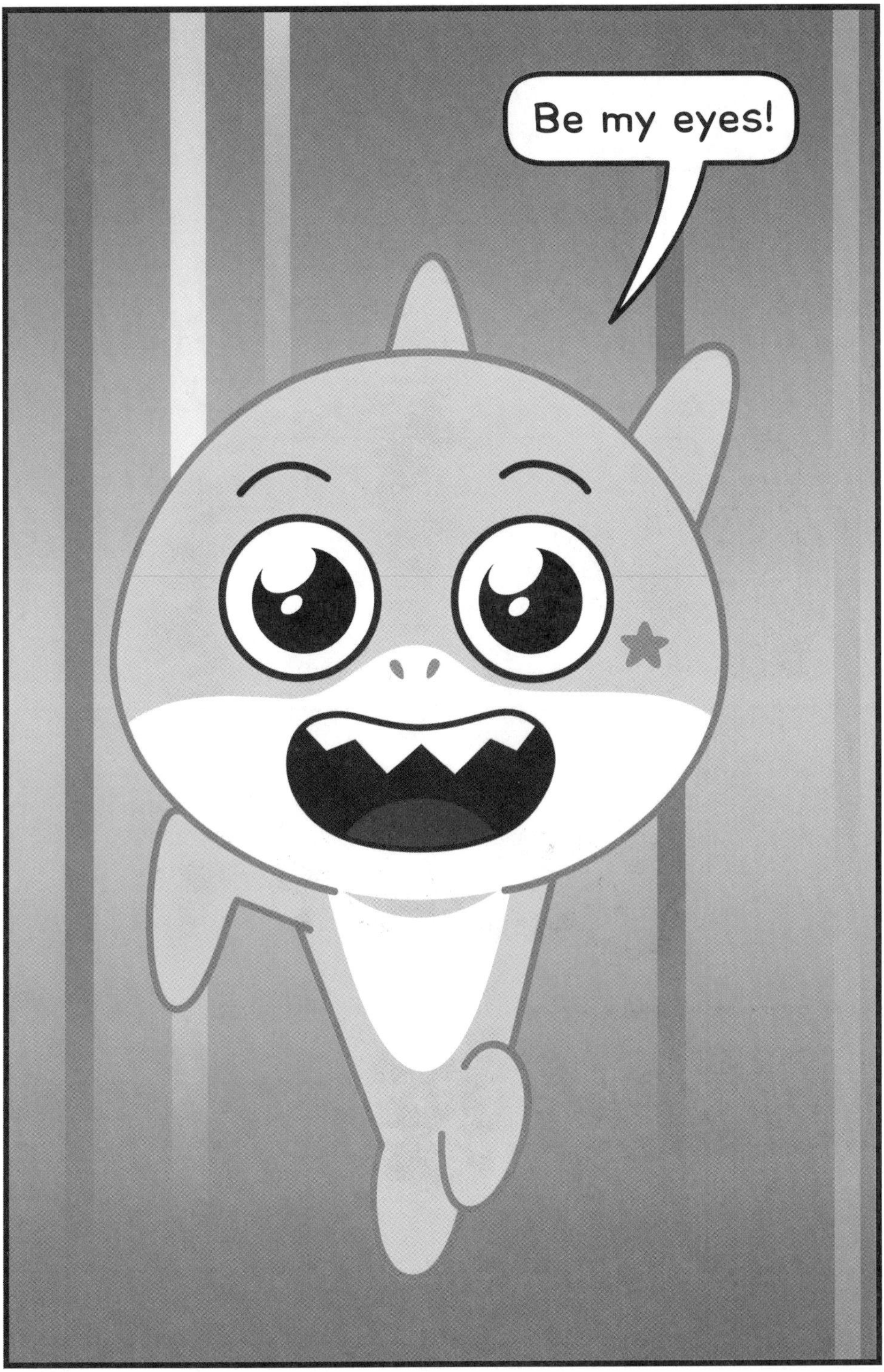
Be my eyes!

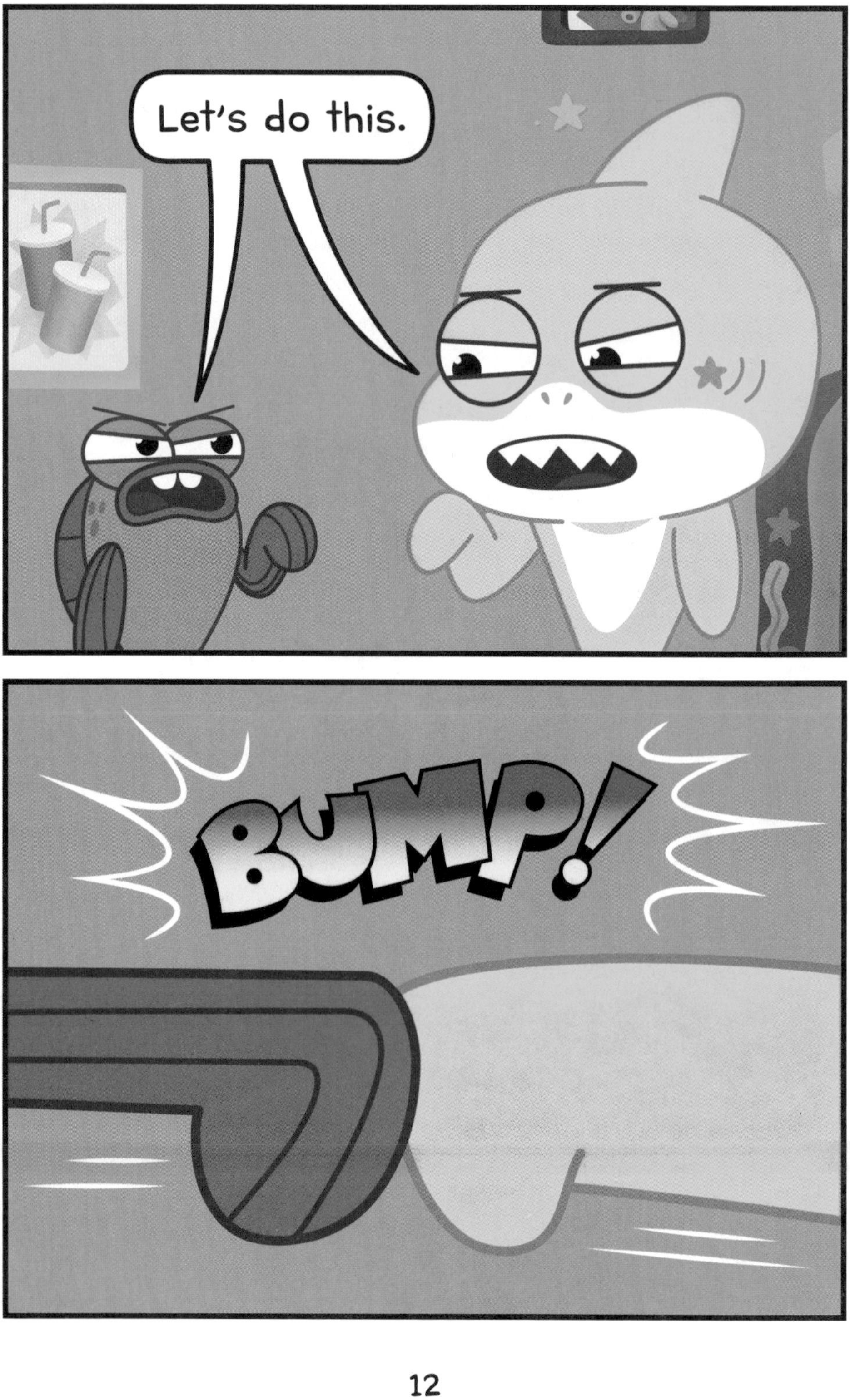
Let's do this.
BUMP!

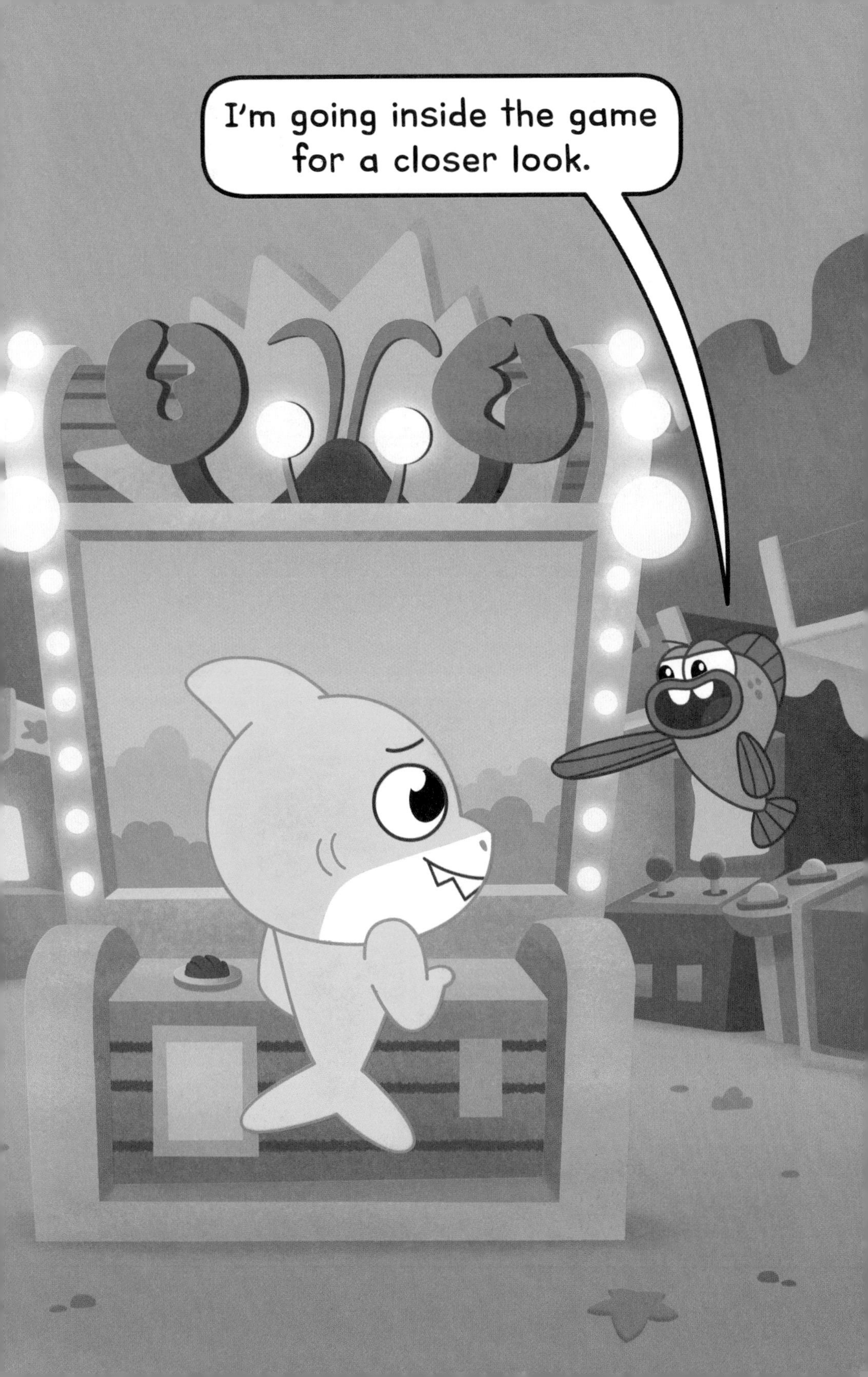
I'm going inside the game for a closer look.

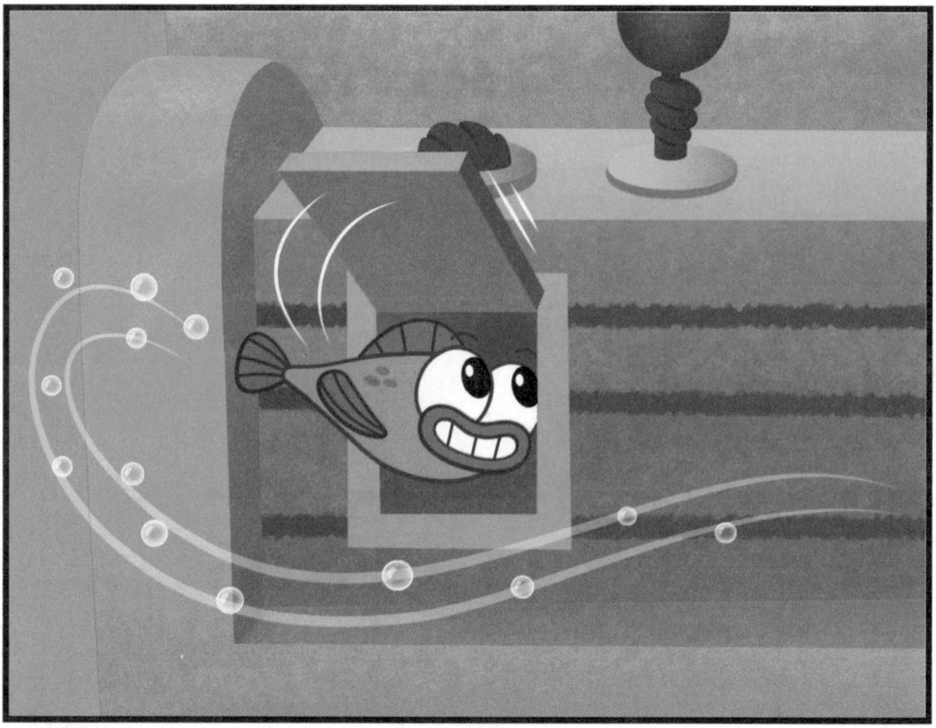

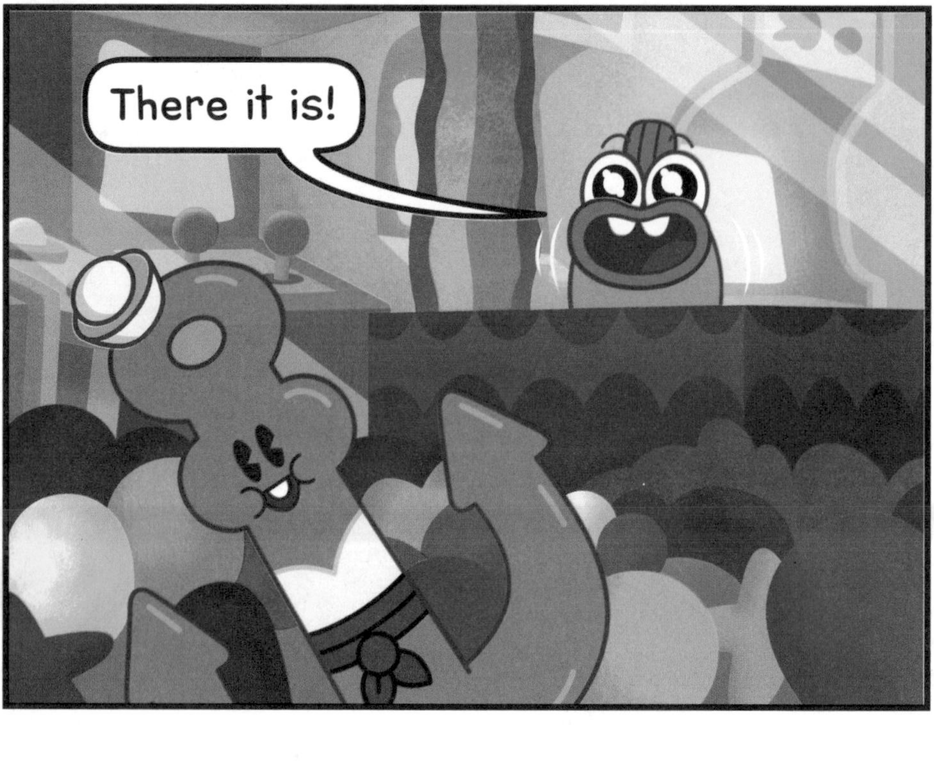
There it is!

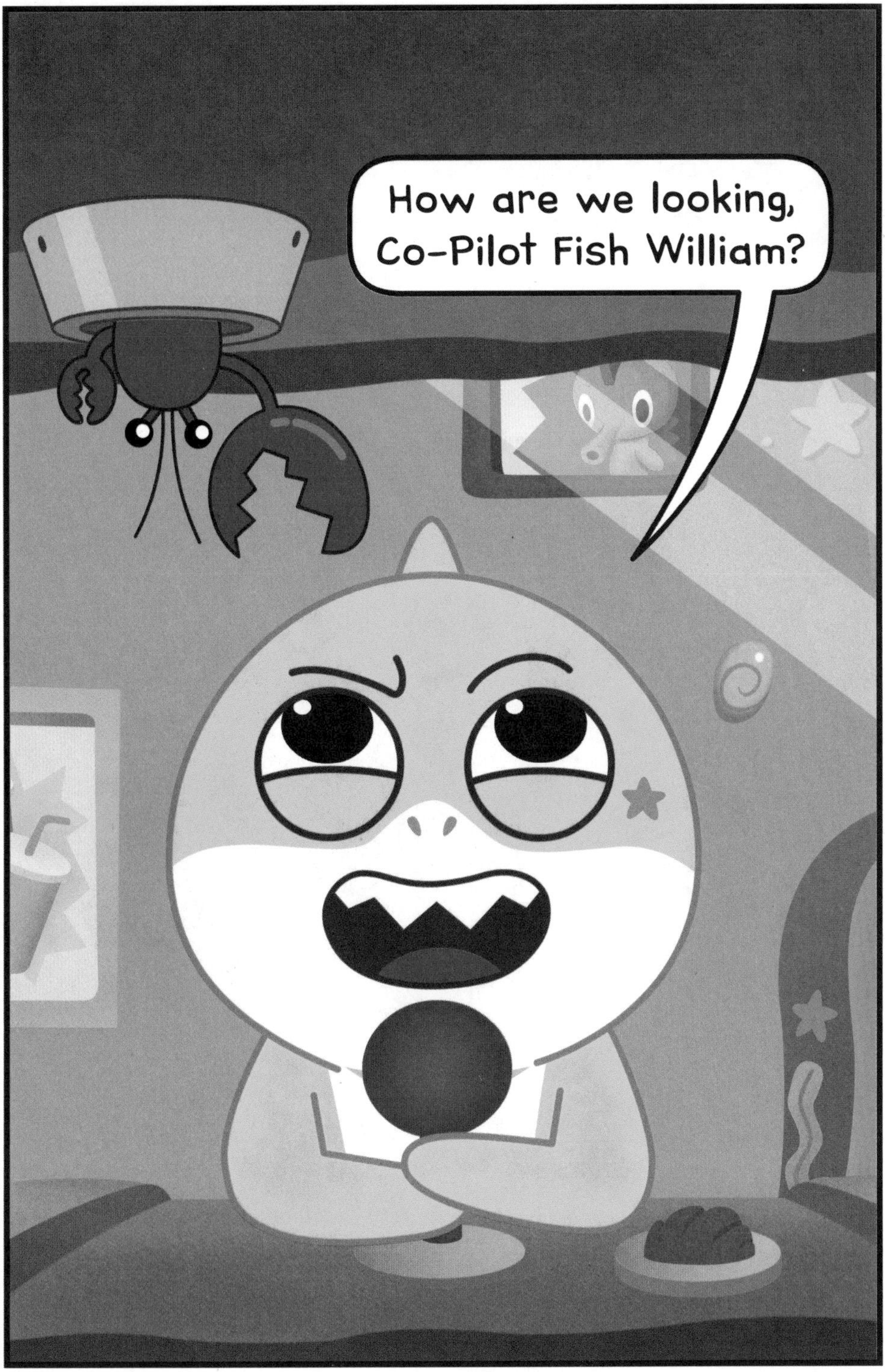
How are we looking, Co-Pilot Fish William?

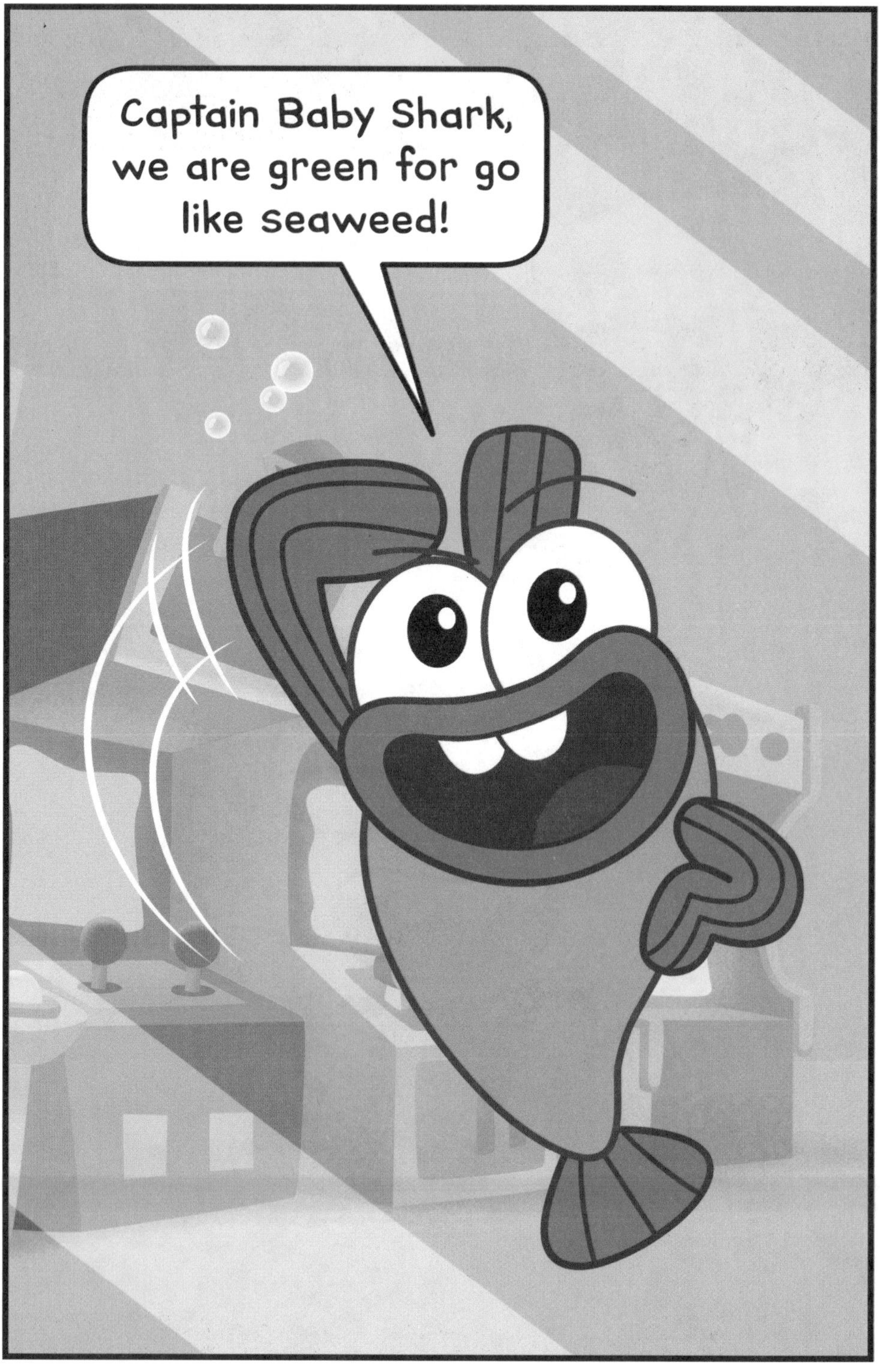
Captain Baby Shark, we are green for go like seaweed!

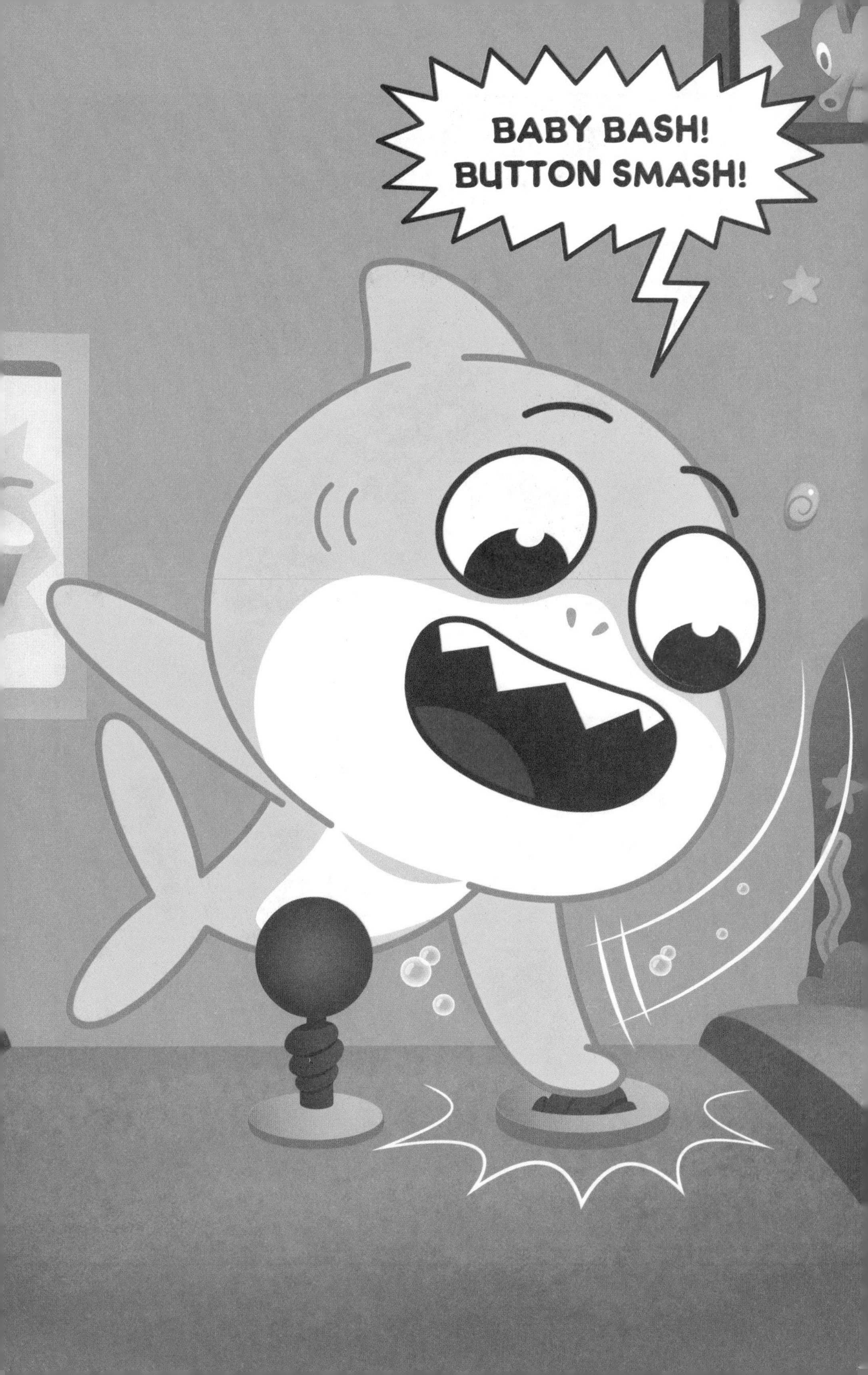
BABY BASH!
BUTTON SMASH!

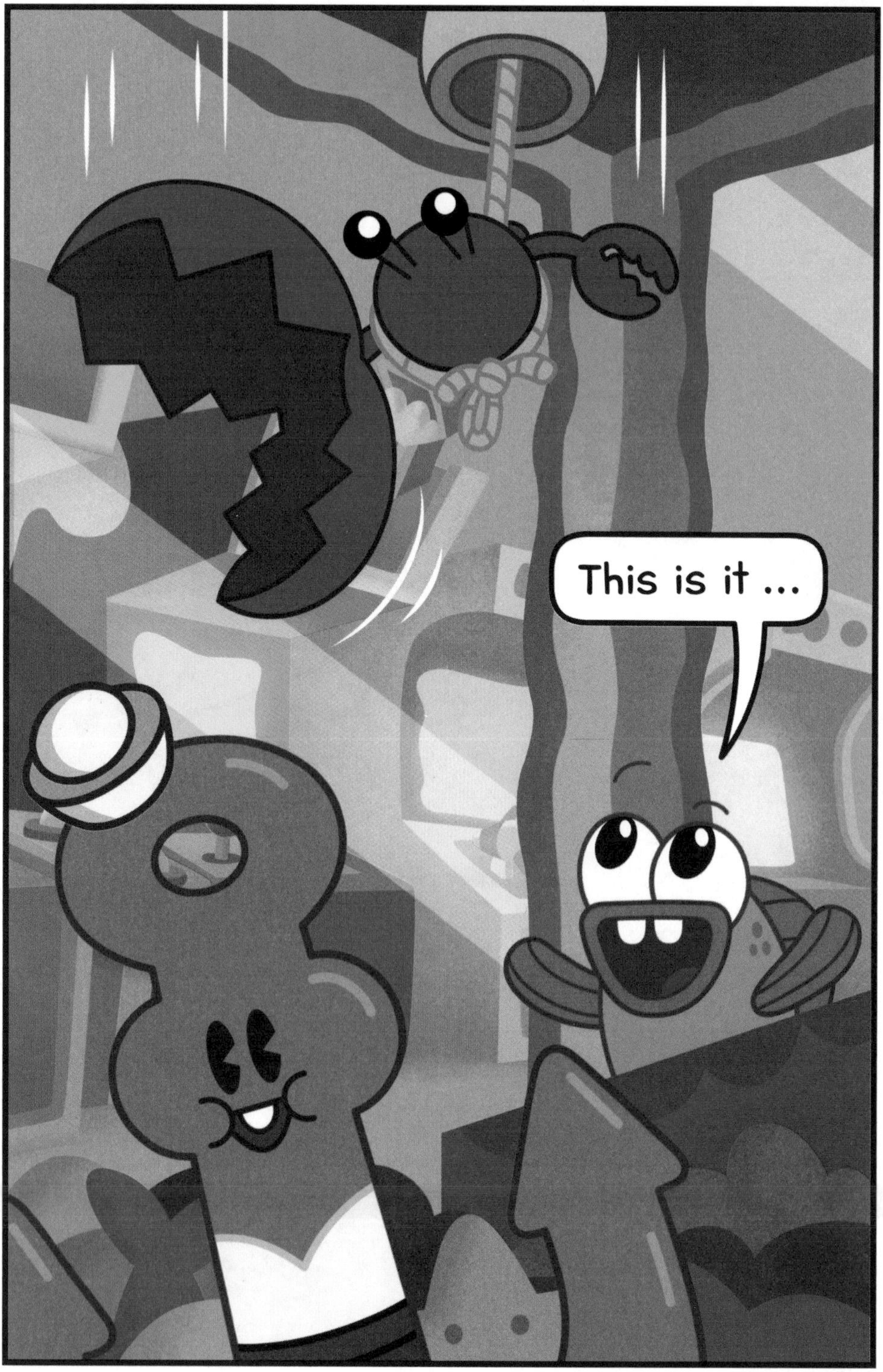
This is it ...

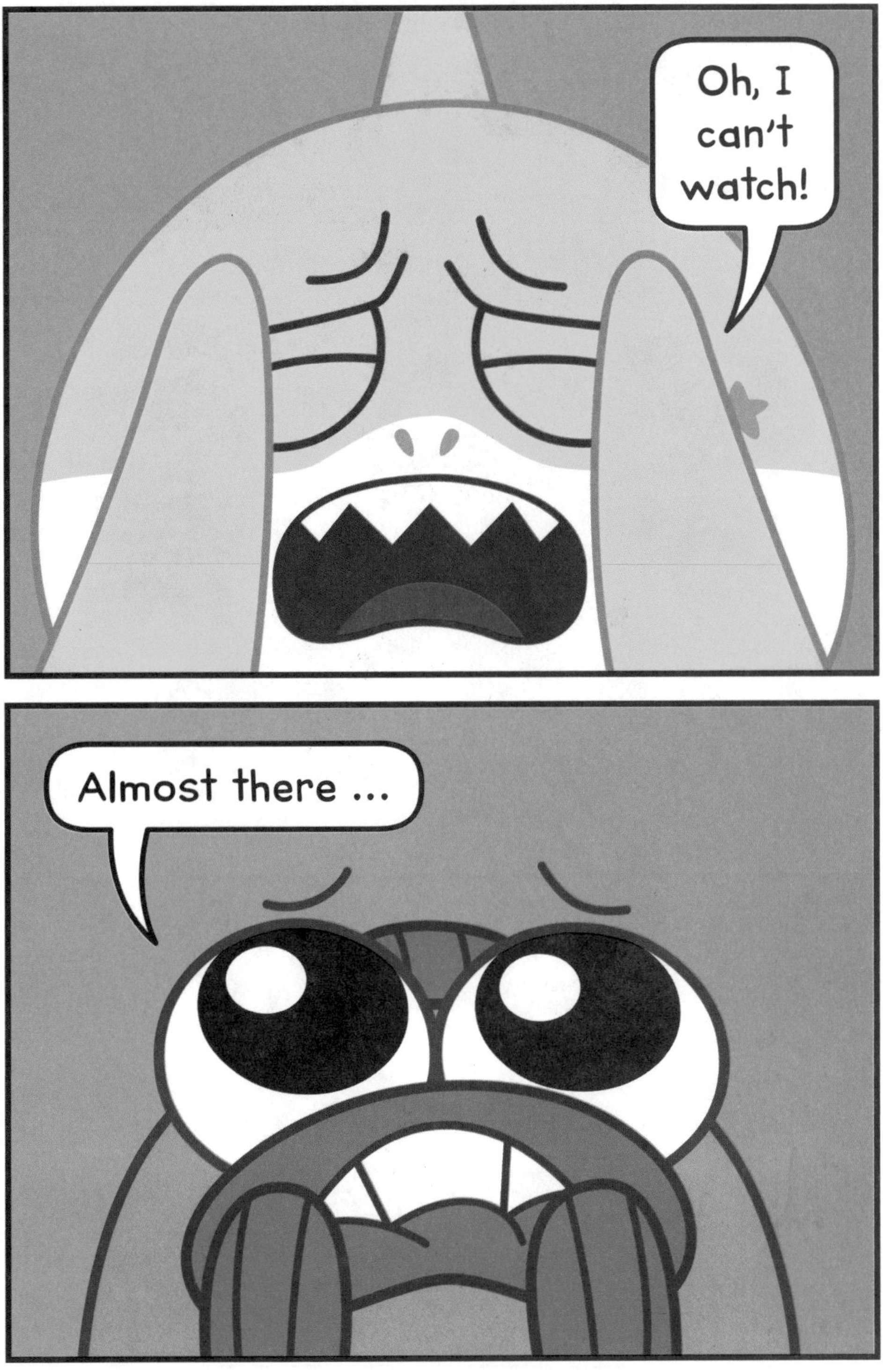
Oh, I can't watch!
Almost there ...

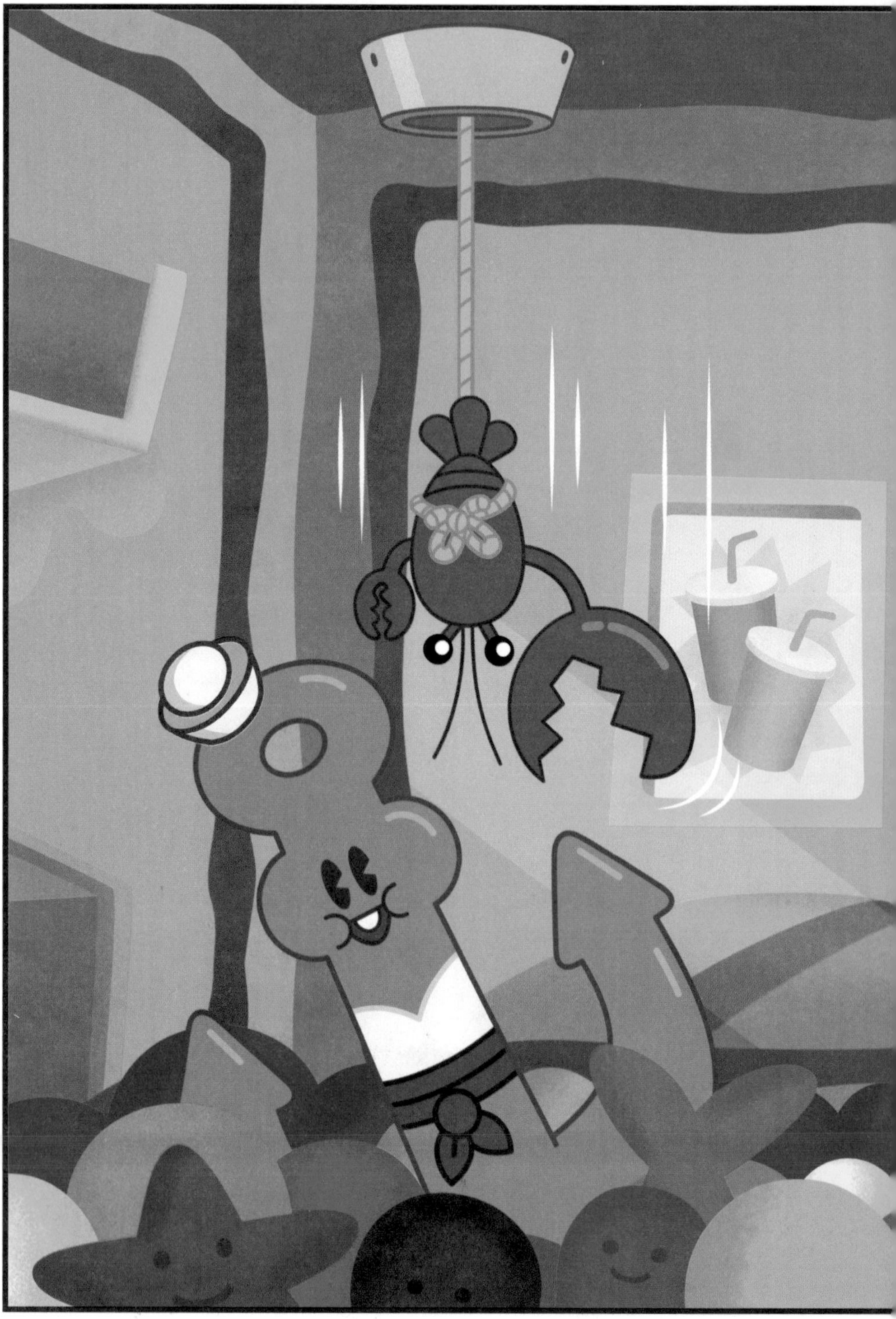

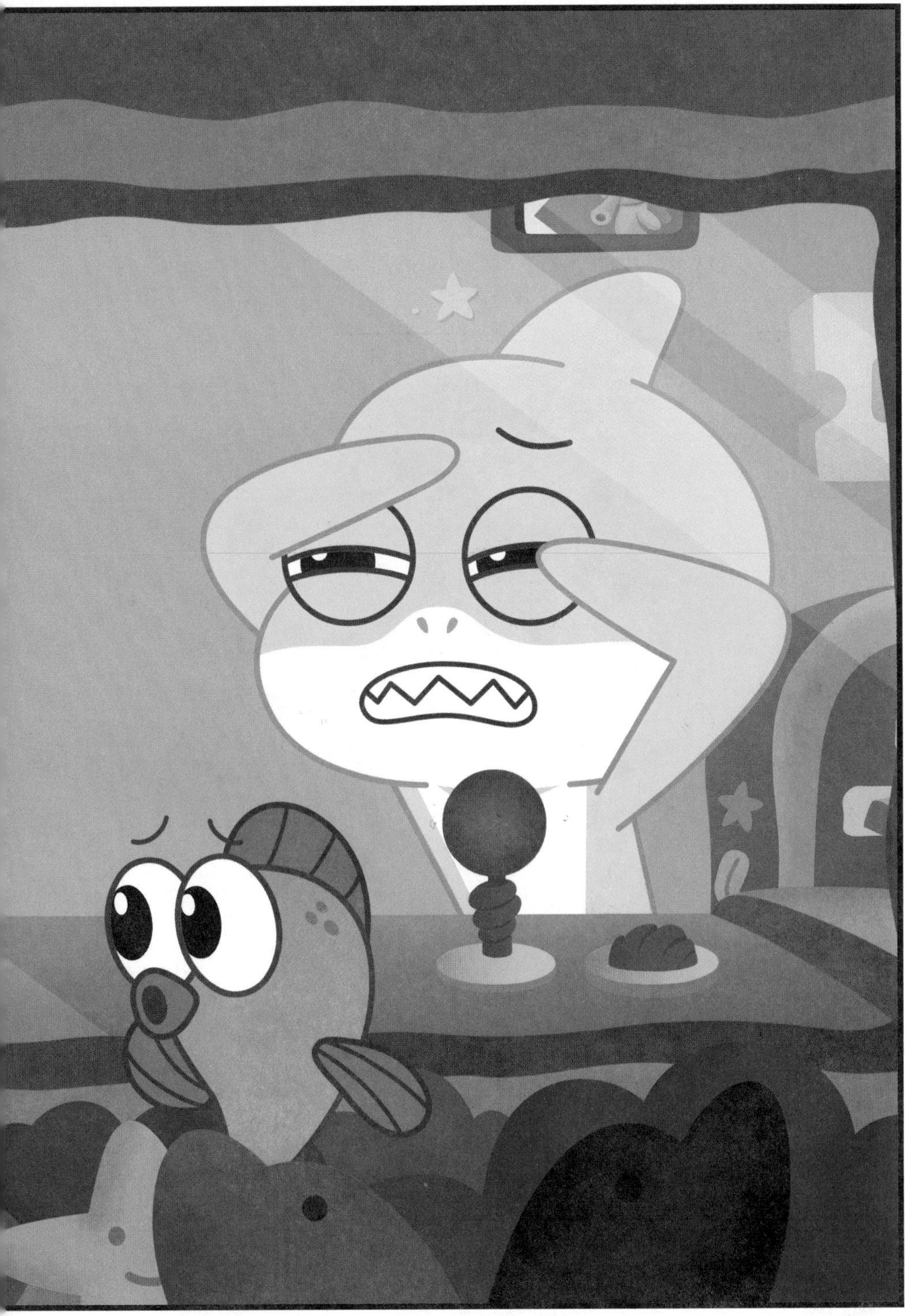

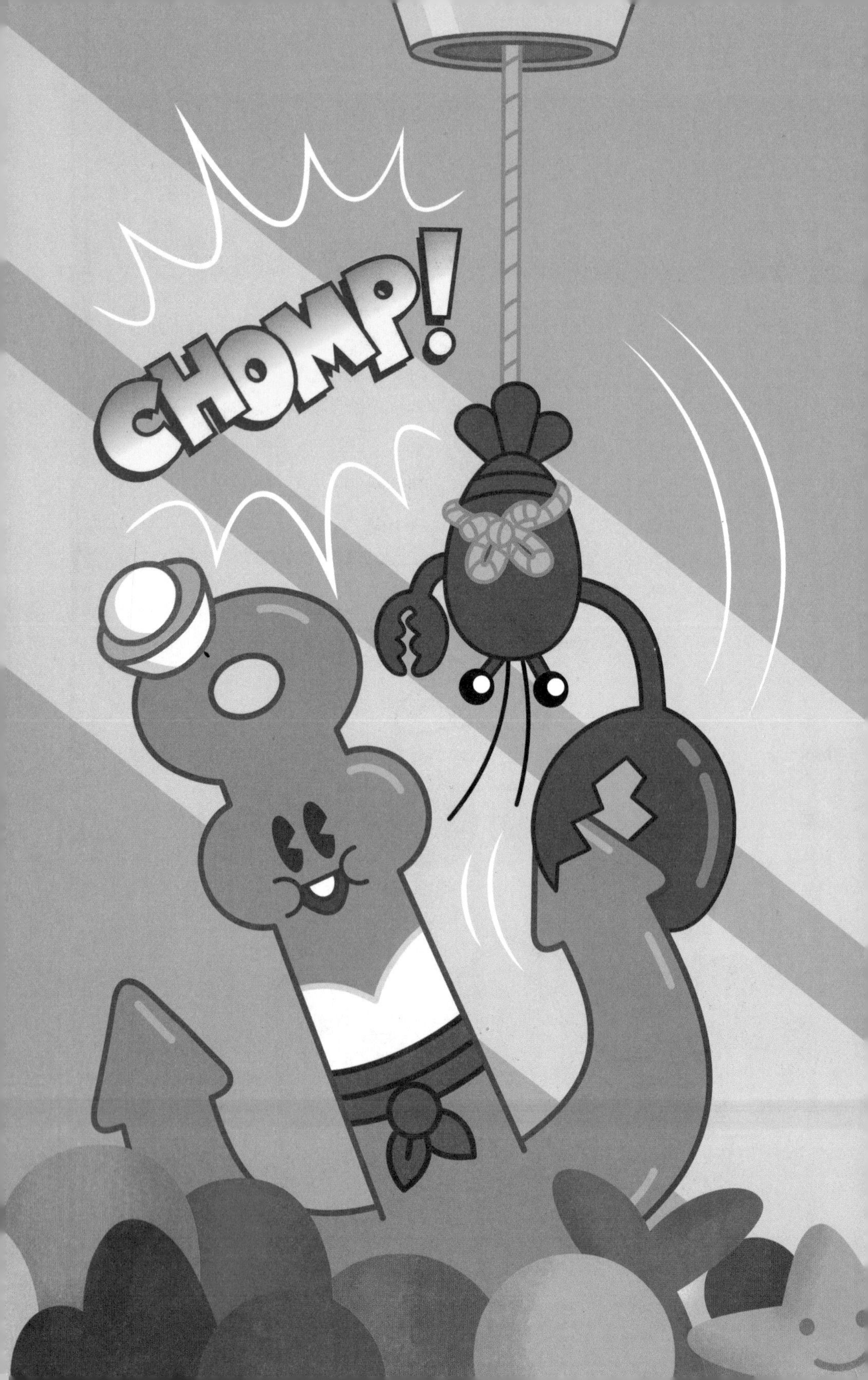
CHOMP!

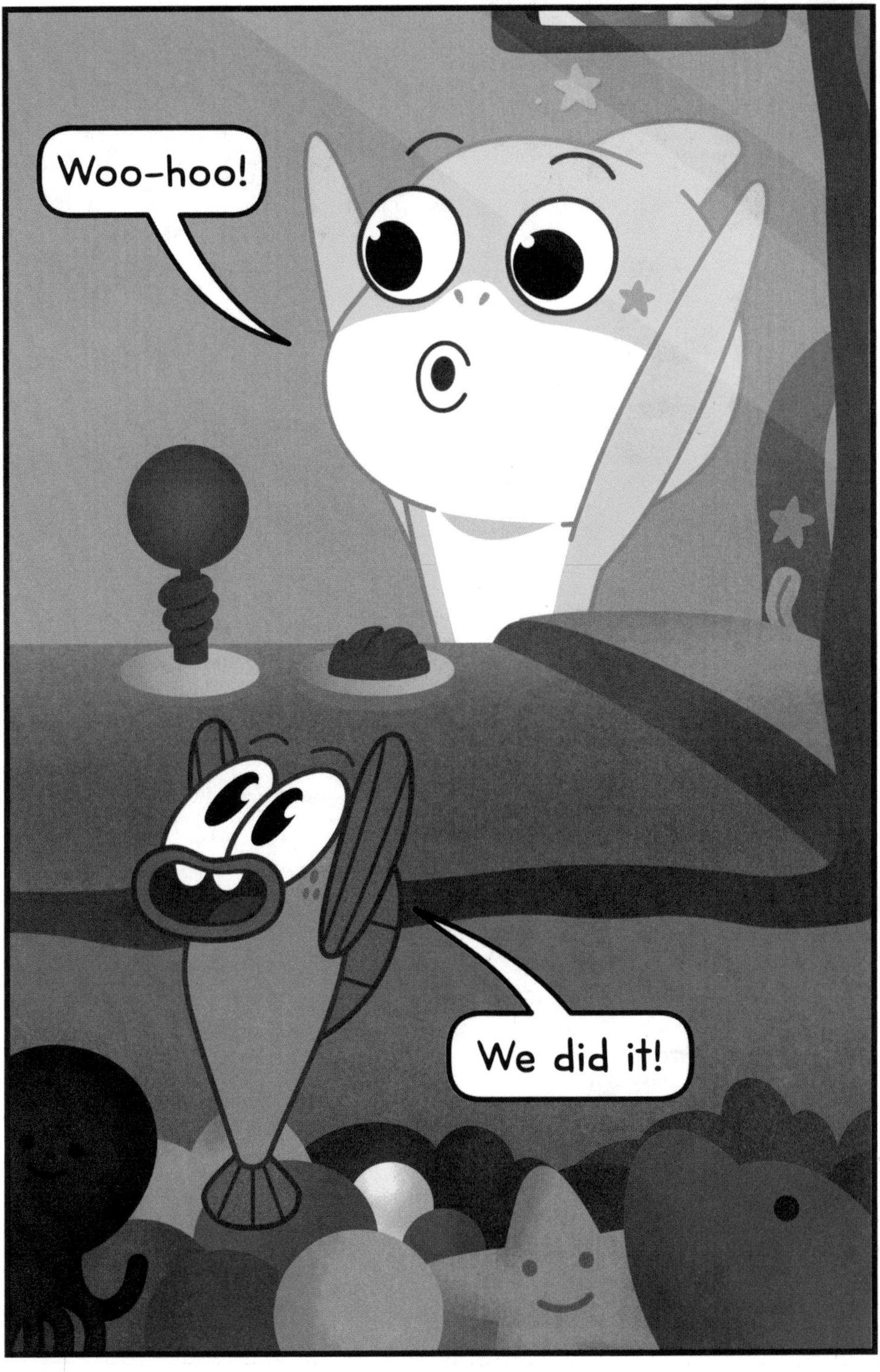
Woo-hoo!
We did it!

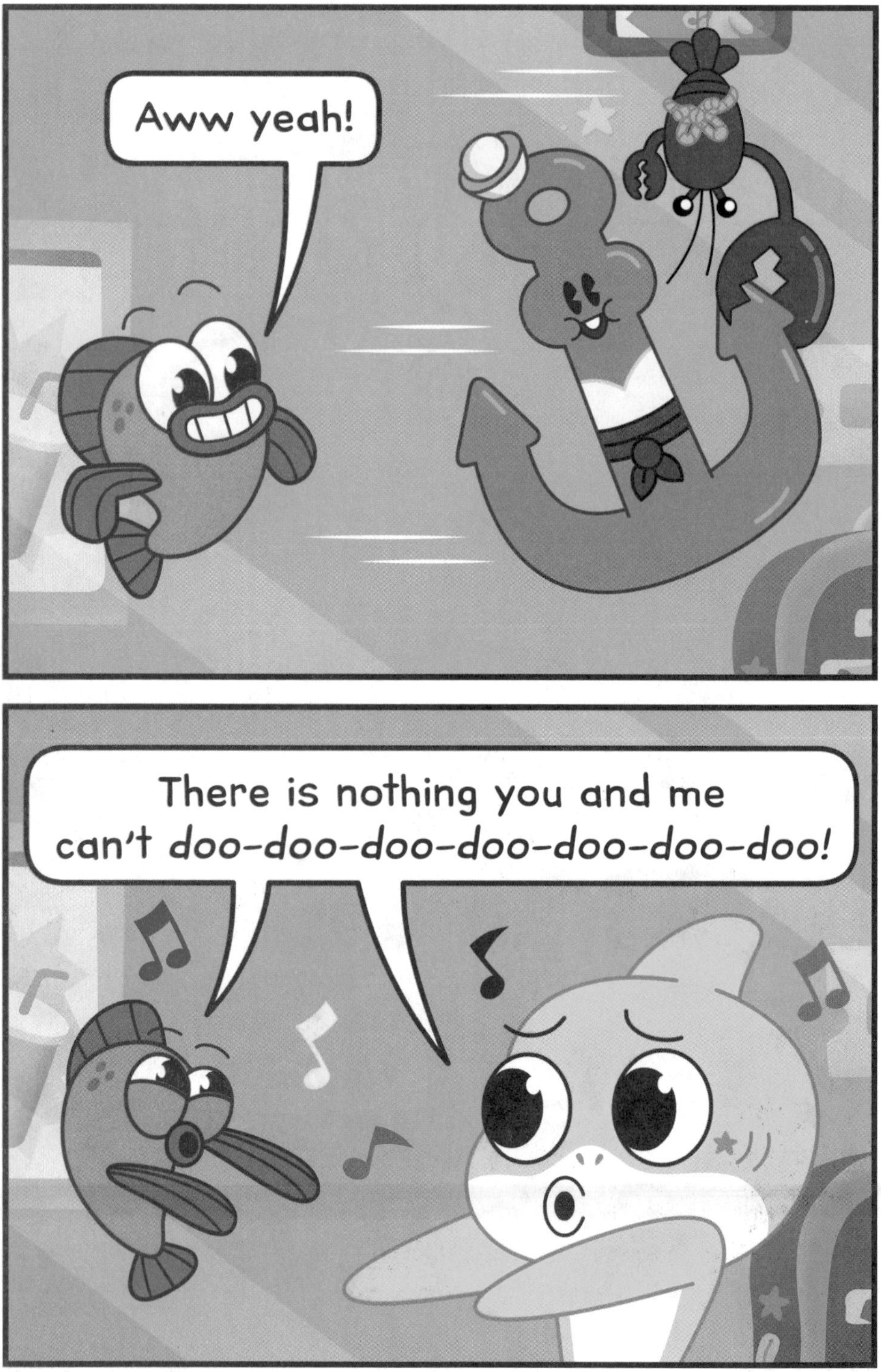
Aww yeah!
There is nothing you and me can't *doo-doo-doo-doo-doo-doo-doo!*

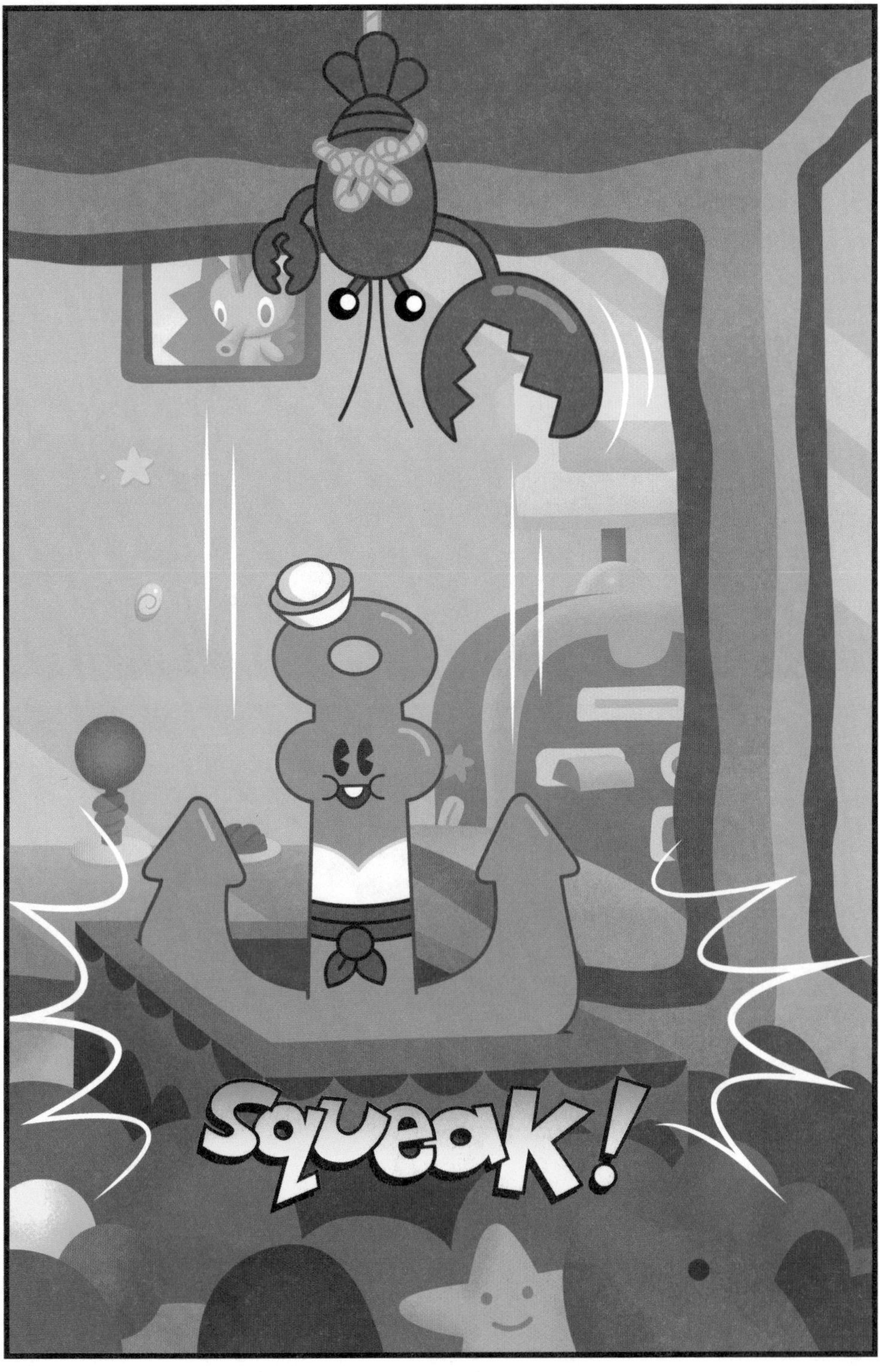
Squeak!

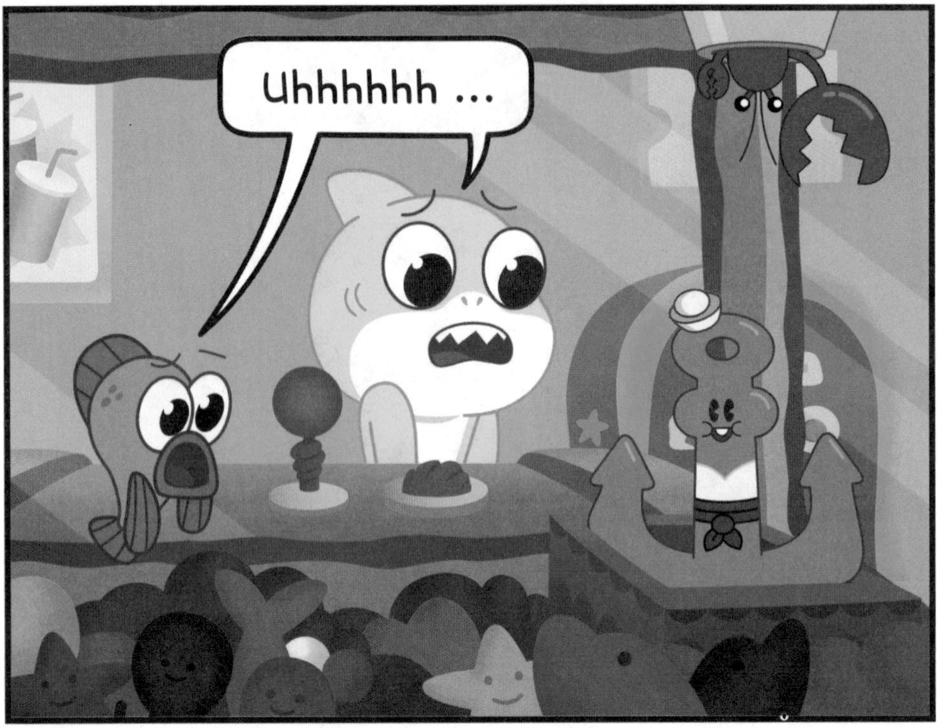
Uhhhhhh ...

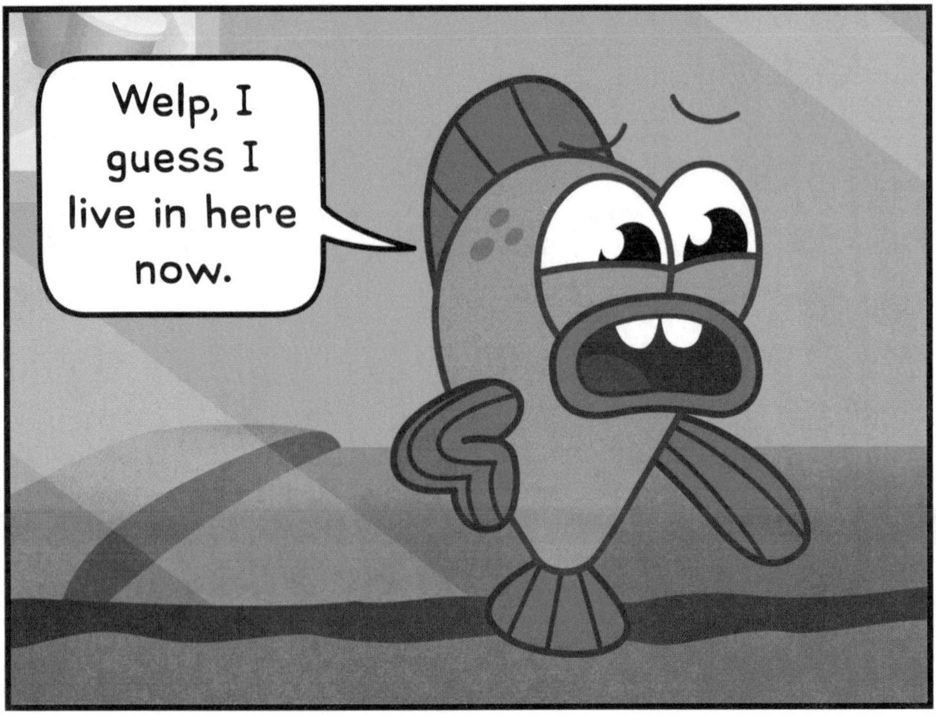
Welp, I guess I live in here now.

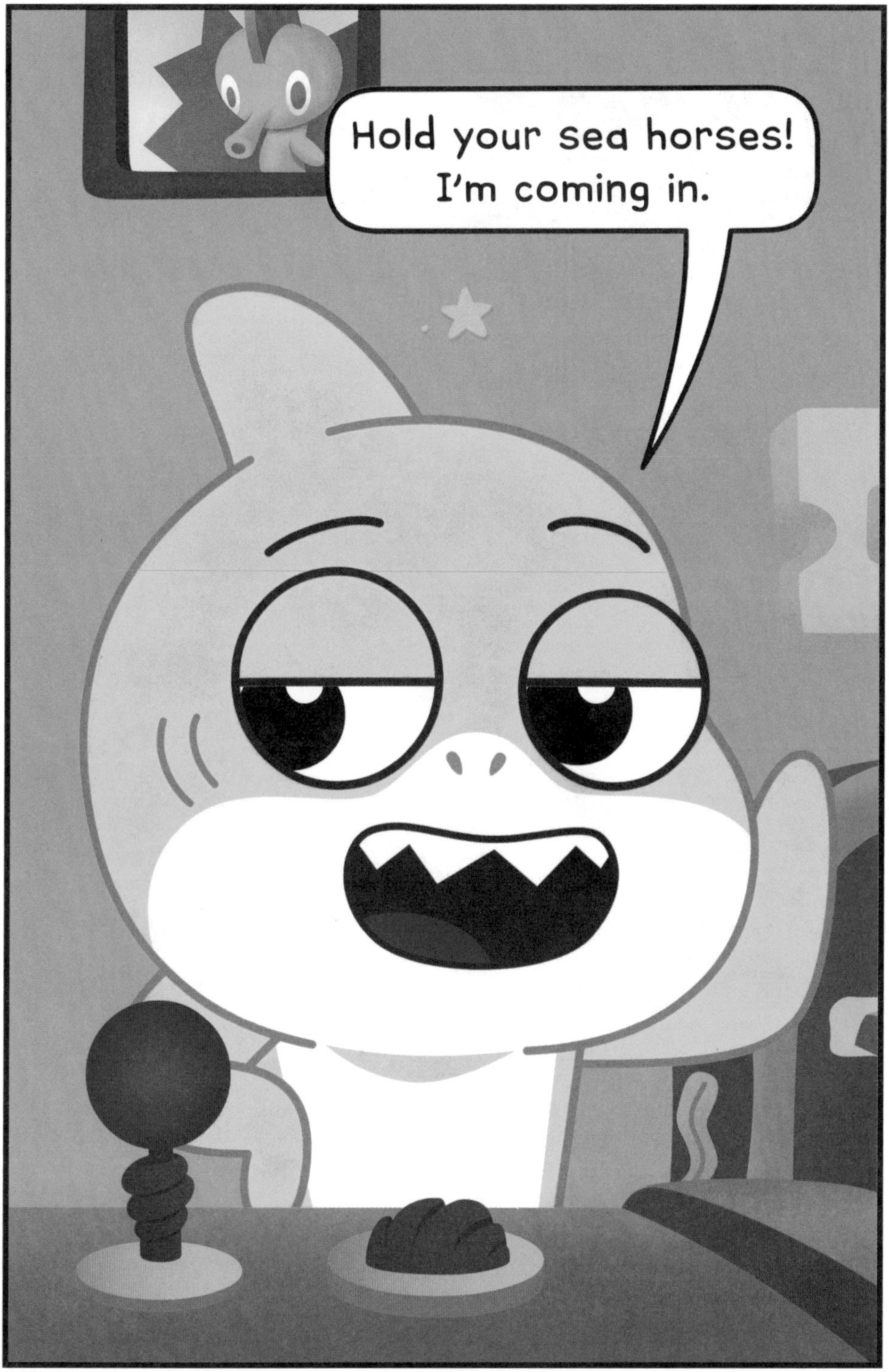
Hold your sea horses! I'm coming in.

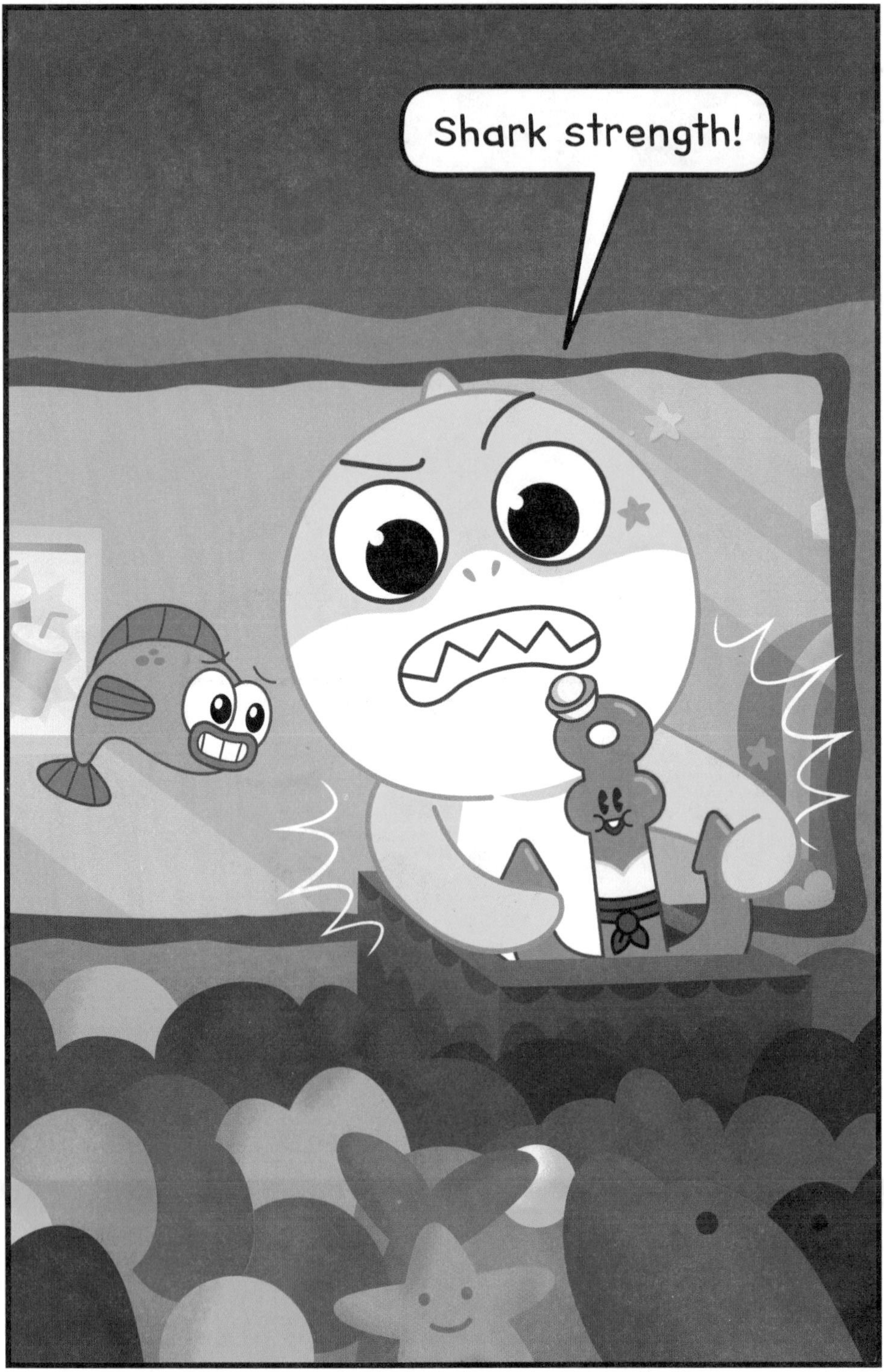
Shark strength!

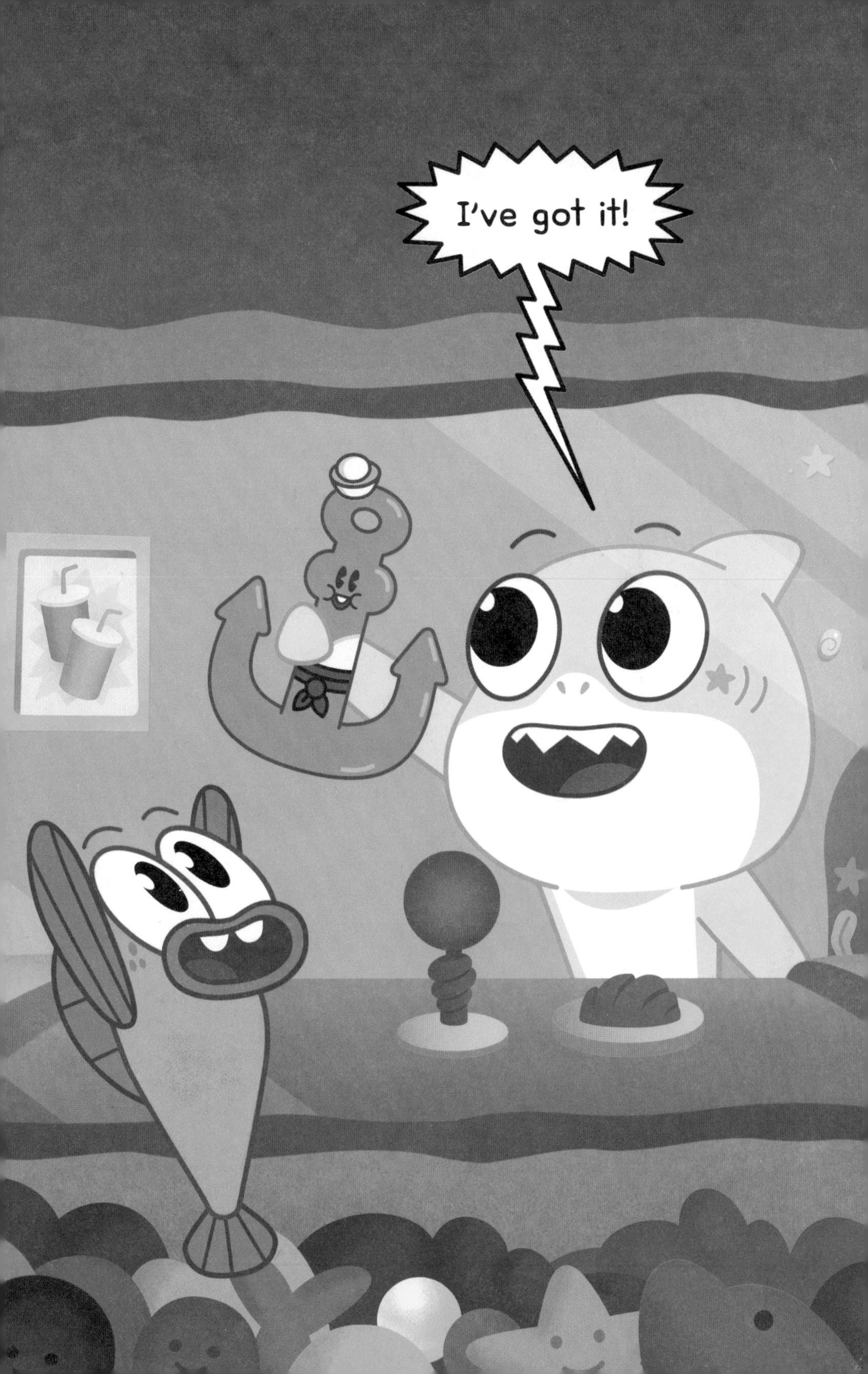
I've got it!

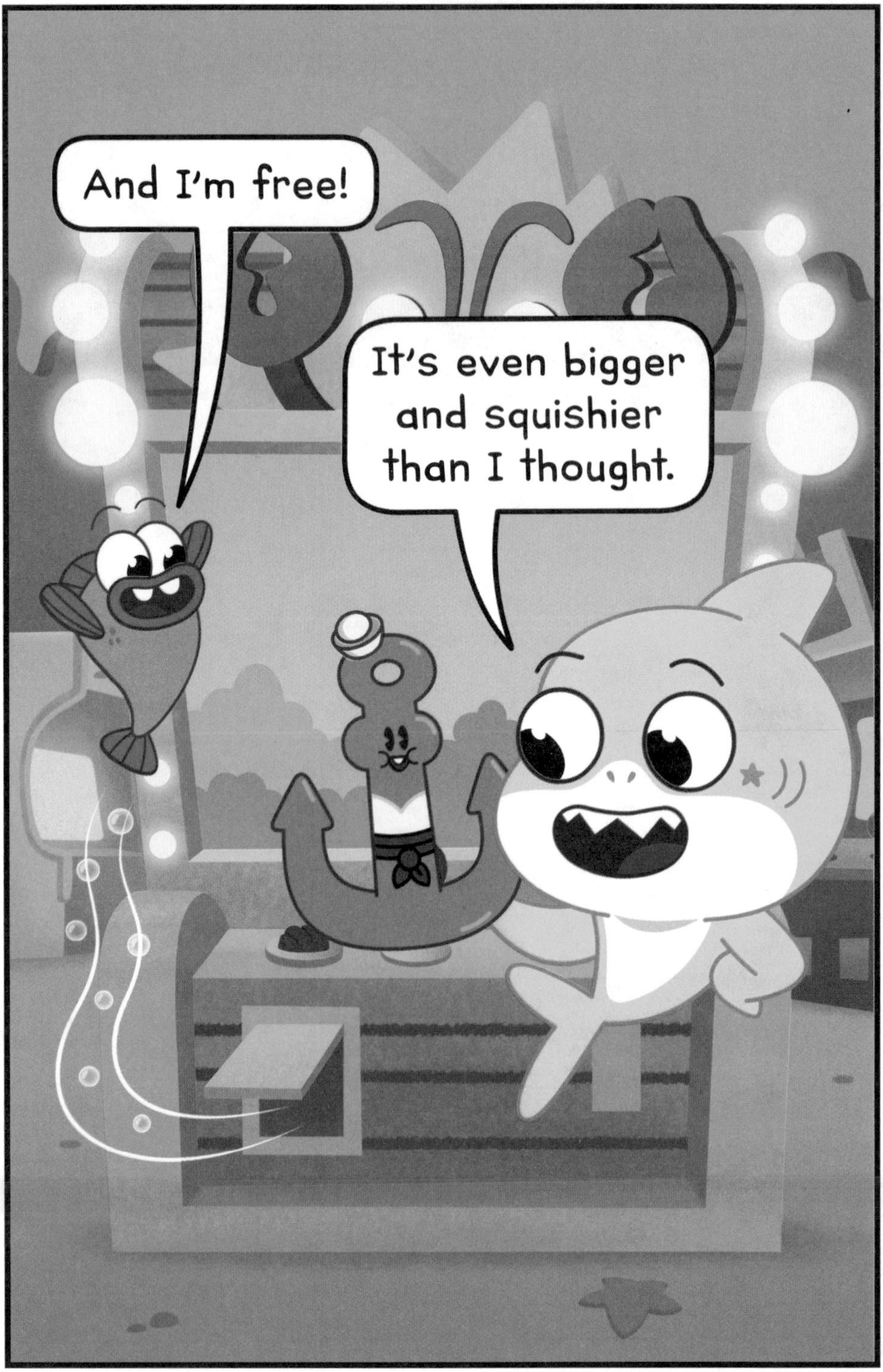
And I'm free!
It's even bigger and squishier than I thought.

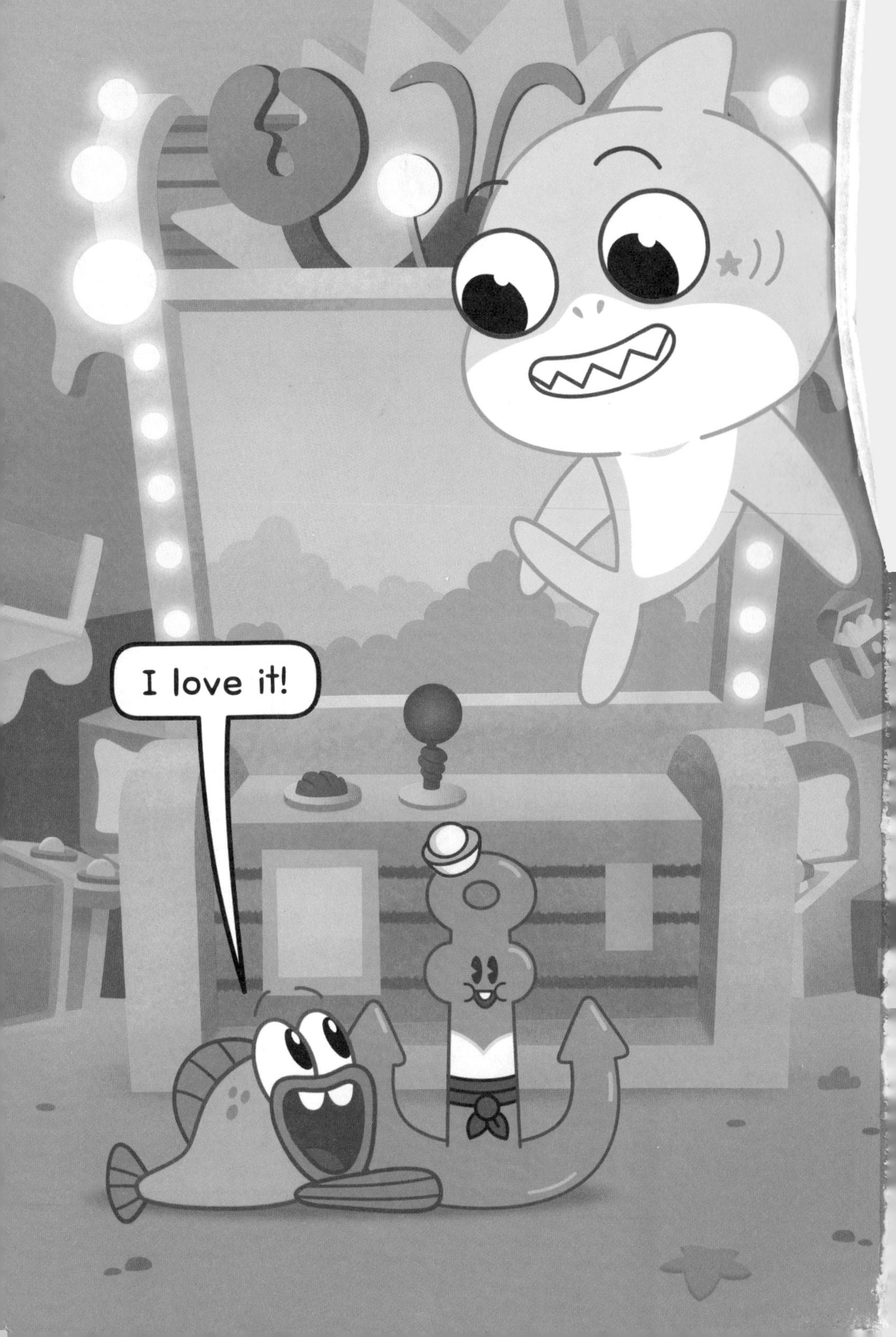
I love it!

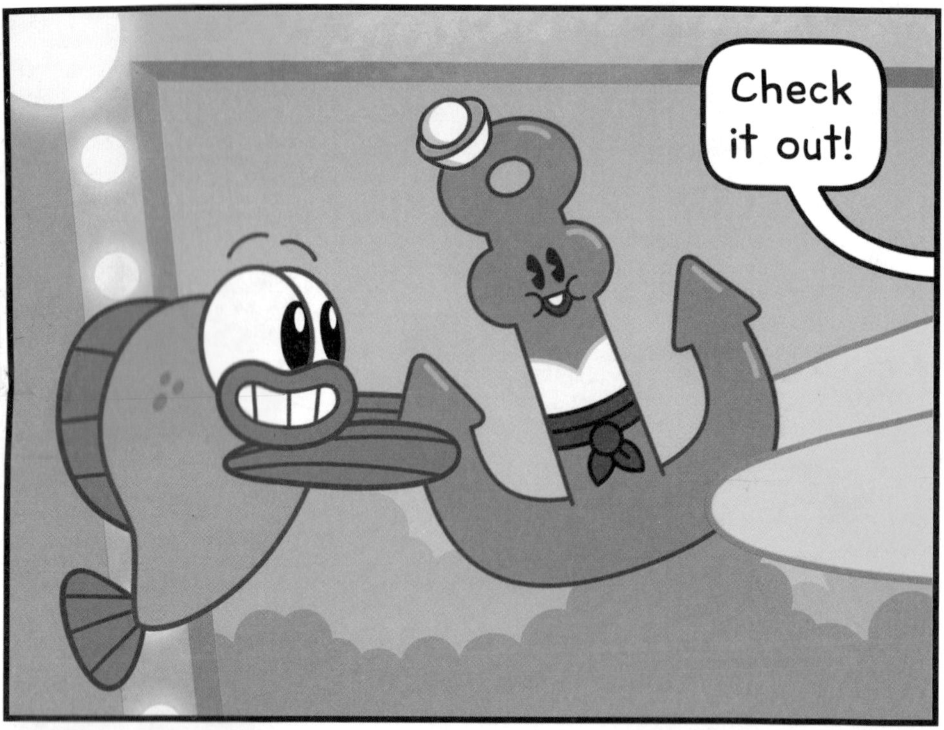
Check it out!

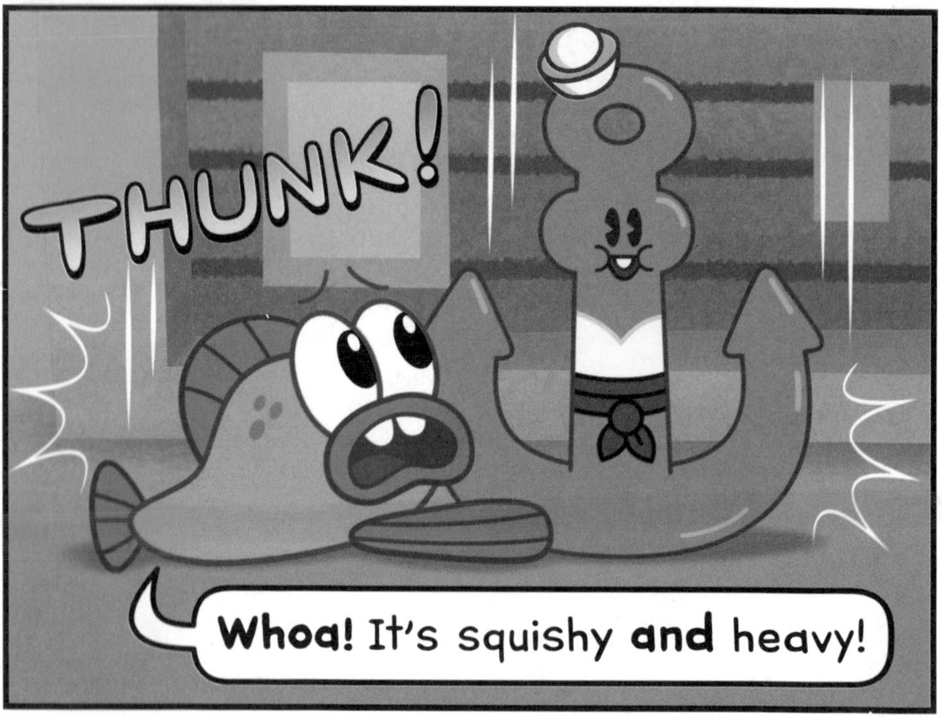
THUNK!
Whoa! It's squishy and heavy!